ALVIN'S SECRET CODE

Also by Clifford B. Hicks

Alvin Fernald Mystery Series:

The Marvelous Inventions of Alvin Fernald
Alvin Fernald, Foreign Trader
Alvin Fernald, Mayor for a Day
Alvin Fernald, Superweasel
Alvin Fernald, TV Anchorman
Alvin's Swap Shop
Alvin Fernald, Master of a Thousand Disguises
The Wacky World of Alvin Fernald

Other Titles:

Peter Potts
Pop and Peter Potts
The Peter Potts Book of World Records
First Boy on the Moon

Alvin's SECRET Code

Code

Clifford B. Hicks

BETHLEHEM BOOKS · IGNATIUS PRESS
Bathgate   San Francisco

For David, Doug, and Gary,
who are more difficult to read
than the most secret of codes.

© 1963 Clifford B. Hicks

Cover art and cover design © Theodore Schluenderfritz

First Bethlehem Books Printing January, 2006

ISBN 978-1-932350-00-5
Library of Congress Control Number: 2005933096

Bethlehem Books • Ignatius Press
10194 Garfield Street South
Bathgate, North Dakota 58216
www.bethlehembooks.com
800 757 5831

Printed in the United States of America on acid-free paper

Contents

CHAPTER 1

The Secret Message

ALVIN FERNALD had a warm, tingly feeling smack in the middle of his stomach.

It was a feeling that started at exactly the same moment every Friday afternoon, just as Miss Peppersmith closed the books on her desk and replaced them neatly between the bookends—each book lined up just so. Always, just at that moment on Friday afternoon, Alvin got the strange little feeling, kind of squishy and warm, inside his stomach, as though he'd just swallowed a miniature hot-water bottle.

Now, walking home from school with Shoie, the feeling was still there. In fact, it had grown bigger. Not even the gray clouds that scudded across the sky, low and threatening with the approach of winter, bothered him; nor the theme he knew he had to write for Monday; nor the knowledge that Mom would be waiting for him at home with a reminder that cleaning his room was "number one" on his list of jobs for the weekend.

Mom never seemed to number the *really* important things to be done on a weekend, such as having a mudball fight with Shoie and Gooey Larson, hunting for pheasant nests in the cornfields on the edge of town, or finishing the library book about spies he was reading. It was called *The Great Spies of History* and was a real bellywhacker of a book. Alvin could hardly wait to get back to it.

But no, cleaning his room would be "number one" for the weekend.

The thought didn't completely wipe away the tingly feeling. Somehow he'd get Shoie to help him clean his room, and they'd still have time to drift out to Maldowski's farm and heave rocks at the hornets' nest.

The nest was in an apple tree in the pasture where Mr. Maldowski kept his prize bull. The bull liked to stand under the tree, just beneath the nest, which was the biggest hornets' nest Alvin had ever seen. For a couple of weeks now, standing on the other side of the fence, Alvin and Shoie had been trying to hit the nest with rocks. They figured that if they succeeded, the hornets would dive bomb the bull below. But so far they had missed.

The warm feeling, for some reason, made Alvin stick his elbow into Shoie's ribs as they walked toward home. It was a good sharp punch, and Shoie doubled over. Instead of stopping, though, Shoie rolled right on over, did two somersaults across Peevey's lawn, and ended with three cartwheels and a back flip.

"Act your age," said Alvin. Then he grinned and added, "Secret Agent Q-3, that's no way for a spy to behave. A spy has to *un*-draw attention to himself."

Since Alvin had started reading the spy book, he and Shoie were secret agents. Shoie was Agent Q-3 and Alvin was Agent K-21 1/2.

"Got to keep in shape," said Shoie. "You never can tell when I might have to knock off a counterspy."

If there was one thing Agent Q-3 didn't have to worry about, it was keeping in shape. Shoie was the best athlete in Roosevelt School. He didn't *look* like an athlete; he was tall and spindly, half a head taller than Alvin, and seemed to be sort of a loose mishmash of arms, legs, elbows, and knees. Shoie—his real name was Wilfred Shoemaker—was the star of the Roosevelt football and basketball teams, and could throw a baseball farther than anyone in school. If anyone could hit that hornets' nest, Shoie could.

Secret Agent Q-3 did two more cartwheels and ended up walking on his hands across the grass beside the curb in front of Mr. Pinkney's house. Then, carefully, he walked along the edge of the street, one hand in the gutter, the other on the curb. Suddenly he stopped, still balancing on his hands, and stared into the gutter.

"Found one!" he shouted.

"Found one what?" asked Alvin.

"Another tottle bop. I mean bottle top." Shoie

frequently got his words mixed up, particularly when he was excited. "It's a little rusty, but not bad."

"Forget the kid stuff," said Alvin. Actually, he envied Shoie the collection of bottle tops. Shoie now had 7,623 bottle tops. They had been smashed flat with a hammer in Shoie's basement and stored in twenty-one cigar boxes. "Come on, Q-3. Forget the kid stuff." Because it was Alvin who was always getting them into scrapes—and back out again—he pretended that he was much older than Shoie, even though they had birthdays within a week of each other.

Shoie, now purple in the face, carefully balanced himself on one hand and reached out with the other to snatch the bottle top from the gutter. He managed to snag the bottle top all right, but at the same time he accidentally scooped up a stray scrap of paper. Flexing his arms, he gave a mighty heave, flew through the air, and landed on his feet. Then he sat down to look at the bottle top.

"Boot reer," he announced to Alvin, who sat down beside him. "I mean root beer."

Shoie was about to toss the scrap of paper aside when he glanced at it. "What's this, old bean?"

"What's what, old man?"

The two boys frequently called each other "old bean" and "old man."

"What does this scrap of paper mean? Looks mighty mysterious to me."

Alvin looked at the scrap of paper in Shoie's hand.

Suddenly, a sixth sense told him that Secret Agent Q-3 had found something important, much more important than a root beer cap.

On the piece of paper was scrawled a message:

SERIOUS MILLY HIDING THURSDAY. START SECRETS. IVAN HIDING MESSAGE OAK. REMAIN SILENT.

HERMAN

The message didn't make sense—but that's why it *did* make sense to Secret Agent K-21 1/2.

"It's a secret message," he said quietly, trying to keep his voice matter-of-fact. "A message in a spy's secret code."

"Wow!" Q-3 straightened out the piece of paper.

"Don't let anyone see you put it in your pocket," said Alvin out of the corner of his mouth. "You can't tell who might be watching. Pick up a handful of grass and pretend you're putting *it* in your pocket instead."

"A handful of grass? Why would I pocket a handful of grass?"

Alvin was ready with the answer. "There's nothing else to pick up," he said, "so it *has* to be grass."

Shoie grabbed a tuft of grass and stuffed it in his pocket with the paper.

The two agents, trying to be nonchalant, strolled down the sidewalk until they reached the corner. Then

they ran for spy headquarters in the bedroom of Agent
K-21 1/2.

That's how the adventure began. And Alvin
Fernald had a remarkable knack for landing smack in
the middle of adventures.

Alvin was a bit short for a twelve-year-old, and was
far from good-looking. There were more freckles on
one side of his face than the other, which gave him a
slightly lopsided look when you stood straight in front
of him. He had the short blond hair of his father, who
was a sergeant on the police force.

Alvin was perhaps the best-known kid in Riverton,
a middle-sized town in Indiana. His name had appeared in the *Riverton News* numerous times, because
of the adventures he had stumbled into. Somehow,
though, he always came out victorious.

Shoie greatly admired Alvin's thinking ability, and
frequently talked about it as though it were a super-elec-
tronic computer. He called it "Alvin's Magnificent Brain."

"What does the Magnificent Brain have cooked up
for today?" Shoie would ask on Saturday morning. Or,
if they were faced with a problem such as trying to hit
a hornets' nest over Maldowski's bull with a rock from
seventy-five feet away, he'd say, "Put this problem
through the Magnificent Brain and see what clicks out
the other end."

And, of course, it was the Magnificent Brain that
involved Alvin in so many scrapes. Like the time the

Magnificent Brain had suggested that they paint turtles for sale in the local dimestore. They'd found several turtles out along the creek, and set up an assembly line inside Alvin's garage. Everything had gone fine until they'd tried to dip an oversized snapping turtle in a bucket of red paint. At the critical moment, the turtle slipped out of Alvin's hands and fell into the bucket. When Alvin reached in to rescue it from drowning, the turtle grabbed him by the thumb. Alvin ran from the garage hollering bloody murder. That was the day the Woman's Aid Society was having tea next door at Mrs. Gooley's house, and the women were just coming down the front walk full of tea and gab. The turtle finally let go of Alvin's thumb, and when Alvin heaved it away with a howl, it happened to land on Mrs. Osterback's head, spattering red paint in every direction. The *Riverton News* carried a story under the headline RED SNAPPING TURTLE DROPS IN ON AID SOCIETY MEETING.

Now, the Magnificent Brain had decided they should be spies, stimulated of course, by *The Great Spies of History*. The book was so exciting that he could hardly put it down. Last night he had read the chapter on "Spies of World War II" in the dim glow of a flashlight, with his head covered by a blanket, after his mother had insisted that he turn off the light and get some sleep. Now, the Magnificent Brain knew that Alvin just *had* to be a spy. Thus was born Secret Agent K-21 1/2.

As Q-3 and K-21 1/2 walked in the door, Alvin's mother called from the kitchen, "Is that you, Alvin?"

"Yes, Mom." Alvin turned and whispered to Shoie, mimicking his mother's voice, "Number one on your list for the weekend is cleaning your room."

"Number one on your list for the weekend is cleaning your room," called his mother.

"Yes, Mom."

"I want you to do it right now, before you get involved in anything else."

"Yes, Mom."

"There are some cookies out here to give you strength for the job."

Alvin and Shoie went to the kitchen. Mrs. Fernald was standing by the oven, holding out a plate of cookies. She was a pretty woman, with eyes that were surprisingly clear and blue. Looking into them, Alvin frequently had the feeling that Mom knew a great deal more about what was going through the Magnificent Brain than *he* did—almost as though she were a mind reader. Sometimes, it made him a bit nervous.

The Secret Agents each took five cookies and headed upstairs for Alvin's room. At the top of the stairs the Pest was sitting, a football snuggled tightly under her arm, so tightly that it seemed to be part of her small body.

The Pest's real name was Daphne, but Alvin had called his sister the Pest for as long as he could remember. She was eight years old, and because she had always thought Alvin was the greatest, she wanted to be a boy, too. Dressed in Alvin's outgrown blue jeans, she carried a football or baseball wherever she went, and left her fancy dolls to gather dust on the shelf in her closet. But even the way she dressed couldn't hide the fact that she was a girl, for she had a round little face with a slightly turned-up nose and long golden curls that were tied by a ribbon into a ponytail. When she rode Alvin's bike (which she did whenever she could), the ponytail streamed out behind like a flag in the wind.

"Hi, Alvin," she said. "What're you going to do?"

"Man stuff," said Alvin, climbing around her.

"Can I help?"

Down deep, Alvin really liked his little sister. But her turned-up nose was always turning up in his business and this was a continual source of irritation between them.

"Nope."

Before Alvin could close the door to his room the Pest slipped inside.

"Mom says you have to clean your room, number one," she said.

"I'll number one you!" he said, pretending to threaten her.

"I'll clean your room if I can stay," she pleaded.

Alvin was tempted. The sooner they cleaned the room, the sooner they could try to solve the secret code in Shoie's pocket.

"Let 'er stay," said Shoie. He wouldn't admit it, but he enjoyed having the Pest around, mostly for laughs.

"Okay," said Alvin. "But you're going to do most of the work. We have secret business to tend to—maybe involving the H-bomb."

"Oh, Alvin," said the Pest admiringly. "Are you really going to make an H-bomb?" She thought her brother could do anything.

Alvin grinned. "Pick up anything under the bed," he ordered, "while I take care of the rest of this stuff."

"Under the bed," she said, "while you take care of the rest." The Pest had the habit of repeating almost anything that was said to her. Alvin sometimes had the feeling that he was hearing a tiny high-pitched echo of his own voice.

On his bed Alvin made a stack of everything that was out of place: a half-built model plane, two pairs of dirty socks, four springs from an old mattress (which he planned to strap to an old pair of shoes and go bouncing down the street), a tube of glue—minus the lid, of course—a snarl of kite string, a wheel from a baby carriage, a jar of pickles which he'd forgotten to return to the refrigerator, his detective mustache, and two burnt-out television tubes.

On one corner of his desk he placed the jar of pickles and the mustache—which might come in handy in his role as Secret Agent K-21 1/2. Carrying a chair into his closet, he climbed up on it and removed from the top shelf an extra blanket which his mother stored there. Then Shoie handed up the stuff from the bed, and Alvin placed it as far back on the shelf as he could reach. When he replaced the blanket, he tried to be careful, but he heard the wing of the model plane crunch. Well, he'd have to fix it later. It didn't seem quite as important, just now, as it had when he'd started to build it.

Alvin was sure that his mother knew what happened to the stuff he picked up when he "cleaned his room," but she never said a word about the back of the top shelf. Occasionally, Alvin would have to clean off the shelf, behind the blanket, to make room for more stuff.

As he climbed down, the Pest was just kicking his bedroom slippers and sneakers under the bed far enough that they wouldn't show.

"Ready?" asked Shoie, who had flopped down on the bed. "Can we take a look at this secret message now?"

"Okay, Q-3." Alvin sat down beside him and held out his hand for the paper.

"Can I be a Secret Agent, too?" asked the Pest.

"No. This is a man's work."

"Please," she pleaded, "give me a secret name."

Alvin ignored her. By now the Magnificent Brain was analyzing the mysterious words on the secret paper.

And, indeed, they *were* mysterious. No one said anything for a full minute, as the three of them huddled over the paper.

"Maybe it's something one of the other kids dropped," said the Pest helpfully.

Alvin gave a snort of disgust. "Take a good look. Does that look like a kid's writing or what a kid would say?"

> SERIOUS MILLY HIDING THURSDAY. START
> SECRETS. IVAN HIDING MESSAGE OAK.
> REMAIN SILENT.
>
> > HERMAN

"What could it mean?" asked Shoie, unconsciously lowering his voice.

"It means a secret message, that's what it means."

"But what does the *message* mean?" asked the Pest.

The Magnificent Brain clicked. "You've got to *analyze* these things. You can't break a secret code in three minutes. It says so in the spy book."

Alvin took the message to his desk, sat down, and turned on the desk lamp. With the other two leaning over his shoulder, he held the paper close to the light.

"What're you doing, Alvin?" whispered the Pest.

"Seeing if there's any invisible ink on the paper. If there is, probably the light or heat from the lamp will bring it out."

All three waited expectantly, but nothing happened.

"Let's see if we can break the code," said K-21 1/2. He copied each of the words in the message into a list on a sheet of paper. "Anything strange strike you about these words?" he asked.

" 'Hiding' and 'secrets' make it sound like a spy message," offered the Pest.

"Ivan is a Russian name," offered Q-3. "Sounds like a Russian is hiding a message in an oak tree somewhere around here."

Alvin thought for a minute. "Yes," he finally announced with authority, "this is a secret message, probably from one Russian to another. Next question is, why should a Russian spy be operating in Riverton?"

"I know!" said Shoie, excitedly. "The new defense plant on the edge of town!"

The new factory had brought a lot of jobs and money into Riverton. But even those who were working in the plant didn't know for sure what they were making. Small, delicate machines of some kind, but no one knew what they were used for after they were shipped out of Riverton, except that they had something to do with rockets.

"You're probably right," said Alvin. "I'll bet we've stumbled onto a spy ring that is sending out the secrets of the defense plant in coded messages."

The Pest gasped. "Stumbled onto a spy ring! What are we going to do about it, Alvin?"

Secret Agent K-21 1/2 stood up straight, the message trembling slightly in his hand. "We're going to smash it!" he announced simply. "We're going to smash the spy ring to smithereens!"

CHAPTER 2

Another Spy?

IT HADN'T been a good night for Alvin. At Saturday breakfast, although he was excited, his eyes were bleary from lack of sleep and he felt as if he had a piece of old wool sweater in his mouth.

It was the coded message, of course. He'd tossed fitfully for hours, the words of the message drifting through his head. Last night, he and Q-3 had puzzled over the message for many hours. Finally, they had agreed to "sleep on it." Trouble was Alvin couldn't sleep.

Suddenly, deep in the middle of the night, the thought had struck him. It was such an exciting—and probably dangerous—thought that he had sat upright in bed, banging his head on the reading-light. Of course! That was it! He had at least a part of the answer to the puzzle!

Now, seated at the breakfast table across from the

Pest, he was so excited that he found himself pouring his orange juice, instead of milk, over his cereal.

"What's the matter with you, Alvin?" asked the Pest. "Are you going daffy or something?" Daffy was one of his sister's favorite words.

"I've found out something about the secret message," he said in a low voice. He poured some milk on top of the orange juice and took a bite of the cereal. It tasted a little funny, but not bad. In fact, it was quite good. "You ought to try this sometime."

"Do you mean you've solved the code?"

"Nope. But I know who's head of the spy ring."

"Alvin! Do you *really*? What are you going to do now?"

"Soon as Q-3 comes over, we'll have a conference about it."

"Can I come to the conference?"

"Nope. This is just for Secret Agents."

She complained bitterly, but Alvin stood his ground. This was work for men, probably dangerous work.

When Shoie arrived, the two Secret Agents went to Alvin's room. Alvin carefully pressed the button in the door frame that cocked his burglar alarm. It wasn't really designed for burglars; it was designed to warn him if his sister tried to come in without knocking.

Alvin turned to Q-3. "I've got part of the answer to the puzzle," he announced.

"You've colved the sold? I mean solved the code?"

"Nope. But I know *who* wrote it, and *why*." Alvin paused a moment for effect. "I think I know who the secret agent is!"

"You mean there really is a spy in Riverton? Who is it, Alvin?"

"Well, Q-3, you've got to use your brain to analyze these things. Think back, now. Where did we find that piece of paper?"

"Why, over on Highland. Between Second and Third."

"And who lives along there?"

Shoie thought. "Why, the Piggots, and the Waggins, and Mr. Pinkney, and the Gruntleys, and ..."

"Whoa. Which one of those four families is unusual in any way?"

"Let's see. I guess you'd say the Piggots are, because all four of the Piggot kids have their second and third toes connected, which I always thought might be kind of helpful when you went swim ..."

"No, no! Not the Piggots. Think again."

"Welllll. Mrs. Waggin dyes her hair. But I don't see what that has to do with spies."

"No, try again."

"Let's see. Mr. Pinkney doesn't have any kids. He lives there alone. And he's mighty proud of his glower farden, I mean his flower garden. Do you remember the time he chased . . ."

"Right you are. Doesn't it seem a little strange that Mr. Pinkney isn't married? And that he lives there alone? And that he's only lived there for three years? And that it was in front of his house that we found the secret message?"

"Yes," said Q-3. "He's a funny guy. But that doesn't make him a spy."

"Think some more. What kind of business is he in?"

"Why, everybody knows he has a little factory out on Maple Street. Dad says they make electronics parts of some kind. He ships them all over the world."

"Right. And he built that factory about three years ago. It's out near the new defense plant. And until three years ago, no one around here had ever seen him before. Isn't that a bit suspicious?"

"Wellll. I guess so ... but he seems a nice enough guy, except for the time he told us to stay away from his garden. Fatter of mact, I hardly ever see him. Don't know much about him."

"*That's exactly the point,*" said K-21 1/2. "My spy book says that a good secret agent will not call attention to himself."

Shoie thought for a moment. "I still don't think he's a spy."

"Let's try once more. Do you remember the day he chased us out of his garden? What were we doing?"

"We were trying to get my baseball. We were playing in that vacant lot next door. You overthrew me at first and the ball went over Mr. Pinkney's high fence."

"How did we get over the fence?"

"We climbed that big tree on the back of his lot and dropped down on the other side of the fence."

"Right. And what *kind* of a tree is it?"

"Let's see. I think it's an oak."

"You're darn right it's an oak, Q-3. *And what does this message say about an oak?*" Alvin dramatically pulled the secret message from his pocket. He read one part of it, emphasizing each word. "IVAN HIDING MESSAGE OAK."

Shoie sat down on the edge of the bed and scratched his head. A long moment passed. "You know," he said, looking up at Alvin, "you know, maybe you're right."

"Of course I'm right. I didn't go into this secret agent business just for kicks. Mr. Pinkney is a secret agent for a foreign power."

Alvin had picked up those words from his spy book.

"What do you suppose he's trying to do around Riverton?"

"I'll bet he knew the defense plant was coming here to Riverton. I'll bet he came here first, and started a little business so nobody would be suspicious. And I'll bet right now he is stealing the defense plant secrets and sending them to that foreign power!"

"Gosh, Alvin! What'll we do? Tell your dad? He could get the police department after Mr. Pinkney."

"Nope. I thought of that. Nobody would believe us. Even though Dad is a sergeant on the police force, he'd have trouble convincing the Chief that we were right. And maybe Dad wouldn't believe us, either. Everybody would think we were just a pair of screwball kids."

"They already think that," said Shoie with a grin.

"I also thought of calling the FBI," went on Alvin, ignoring Shoie's last remark. "But they wouldn't believe us either."

"What are we going to do, then? We can't just let Mr. Pinkney go on stealing all our defense secrets."

"We need *proof.* And there's only one way to get proof."

"How?"

"Solve the secret code."

"But we already tried that. We can't solve it, Alvin."

"We need help. We've got to find someone who can solve secret codes. Somebody who won't think it's a joke."

"But there isn't anybody."

"I think there is. We don't know him, but I'll bet he'd listen to us. There was an article about him in the *Riverton News* on Veteran's Day."

"Who is it?"

"His name is Mr. Link. The *News* carried a whole page of stuff on some of Riverton's famous veterans. It told all about how Mr. Link was a spy during World War II. He operated all over Europe, and he learned lots of the German war secrets."

"Where does he live?"

"In an old house over on Fourth Street. He's an

invalid now, can't get out of bed. He has a housekeeper who lives there and takes care of him."

"What makes you think he'd help us?"

"He knows all about spies. He'd take a look at a secret message and *know* it was a secret message. I'll bet he would!"

"Well, what are we waiting for?" said Q-3. "Let's go!"

Alvin folded the secret message carefully and put it in his pocket. He opened the door. There knelt the Pest. Her ear had been pressed against the keyhole.

"What are you doing here?" asked Alvin angrily. "Can't a guy have any privacy around here?"

"I was listening—all about Mr. Pinkney being a spy, and about going over to Mr. Link's house. And about everything like that." She flipped her ponytail and smiled up at him.

"You're worse than a hidden microphone!"

He'd read all about hidden microphones in his spy book, and when he'd gone into the secret agent business he'd pretended to search his own room for a mike. Now he was as mad at himself as he was at the Pest. Being an experienced secret agent, he should have taken some precautions, like stuffing the keyhole.

"I'm coming with you," said the Pest.

"No you're not," said Alvin. But he didn't have time to stand around arguing with her.

He and Shoie headed around the corner toward Fourth Street on their bikes. Out of the corner of his eye Alvin could see the Pest following them on her smaller bike, her legs pumping madly in an effort to keep up. Alvin stood up and pedalled faster.

He skidded to a stop in front of an old house, shaded by tremendous maple trees. He and Shoie had parked their bikes on the front walk and were heading up the steps to the front porch, when the Pest coasted up the driveway. It wasn't the fact that she was there that irritated Alvin. It was the fact that he was out of breath, and she was scarcely puffing as she pushed down her kick stand and ran over.

"What're we going to say?" whispered Shoie. "We can't just say that we know there's a spy in Riverton."

"Let me do the talking." K-21 1/2 spoke with authority. When he punched the button, they could hear a buzzer sound somewhere in the depths of the house. Footsteps approached the door. It swung inward, and through the screen they could see a small gray-haired lady, dressed in an apron, everything about her as neat and clean as fresh-folded laundry. Unconsciously, the Pest straightened her ponytail.

"Yes?" said the lady. It was a question. She seemed surprised to see three children on the doorstep.

"Is Mr. Link home?" asked Alvin.

"Yes. He's home. But he can't come to the door. Perhaps I could take him a message?" Again it was a question.

"If you don't mind, we'd like to see him on some important business," said Alvin.

"We know he can't get out of bed," put in the Pest.

Alvin kicked her in the ankle. The lady had seen the movement of his leg.

"That's all right," she said, with a gentle smile. "It's quite true that Mr. Link is an invalid. But perhaps you could tell me what you want to see him about. If you're selling tickets to the Boy Scout Jamboree, he has already bought one."

"No. It's pretty important, though."

Just then a man's voice, deep and hearty, boomed from inside the house. "Margaret! I can hear you out there. Whatever those kids want, bring them in here. I want to visit with them."

"Come right on in, children. I'm Mrs. Murphy, Mr. Link's housekeeper. Go right on back to the first door on your right. That's Mr. Link's room."

Alvin stopped in the doorway to the room, blinking a bit, trying to take in the entire room at a glance. It was high-ceilinged, bright with sunlight flooding in from windows that covered one entire wall. The other three walls were completely covered with bookshelves. Never, except in the public library, had Alvin seen so many books. On a table beside the bed was a fancy chessboard, with finely carved ivory chessmen.

The bed sheets were as crisp and white as though the bed had just been made, and lying there under a bright blanket was Mr. Link. It was obvious at a glance that he had once been a big man. He still had a large chest and broad shoulders. His face looked as though it had been carved from rock, with two deep cracks in the rock running from the outer corners of his eyes to his chin. His hair, long and gray, was the only thing in the room that seemed in disorder. Although the blanket covered his body from the chest down, it was obvious that his legs and hips had wasted away until they no longer seemed to fit the rest of his body.

"Come in, children. Come in! Sit down. I've had very little company in several days. Sit down, sit down." His voice, deep and cheery, boomed through the room.

Alvin and Shoie sat down in the only two chairs in the room. That left the Pest standing beside the door. When Mr. Link beckoned her with his hand, she came over, carefully dusted off her blue jeans, and sat on the edge of the bed.

"Well," said Mr. Link. "Well. You children certainly are a welcome sight. I hope you have time to stay for a visit." He raised his voice. "Margaret! Do you have any gingerbread left in that kitchen of yours?"

There was a sound of movement in the kitchen, and Mrs. Murphy promptly appeared, smiling, and bearing a plate of gingerbread. She passed it around, insisting that each take two pieces. Then she disappeared into the other part of the house.

"Now," said Mr. Link. "What can I do for you? I have a boy who mows the lawn, rakes the leaves, and shovels the sidewalk in the winter. My newspaper is delivered by another boy. I already subscribe to too many magazines. And I've bought my ticket to the Boy Scout Jamboree, even though, as you can see"—he gestured toward his legs—"it will be a bit difficult for me to attend. But perhaps you have some other business offer to make?"

"We heard you had been a spy," Alvin blurted out.

Mr. Link gazed at him steadily for a long moment. Then he said softly, "And you came to hear some spy stories?"

"Not exactly," said Alvin.

The man on the bed smiled again. "Well, I'm glad of that. Spying is a dirty, dirty business. It's something that must be done, but I'm glad it's over—at least for me. Yes, it's quite true that I was a secret agent during the war. But that was a long time ago. A long time ago."

"Do you know anything about codes?" asked Alvin, coming straight to the point.

"Oh, it's codes you want to talk about," said Mr. Link. "Now there's a very exciting subject: secret codes and ciphers."

"Secret codes and *what*-fers?"

"Ciphers. What you call codes are, in most cases, really ciphers: complete secret alphabets. Yes, I know a bit about both codes and ciphers. I've written a couple of books on them. They are the most exciting of all mental exercises, a thousand times more fascinating, for example, than chess." He gestured toward the chessboard. "I suppose you kids want to make a secret cipher for your own private use?"

"No," said Alvin. The Magnificent Brain refused to find any easy way into the conversation, so he just blurted out, "We know there's a spy in Riverton. He's stealing the secrets of the new defense plant. We know who he is. And we have one of his secret messages in code."

Mr. Link raised his eyebrows. "Oh? Here in Riverton?" He thought for a moment. "Well, I suppose it's possible."

Alvin had liked Mr. Link from the moment he had seen him. Now, he was sure they'd found a strong friend. Mr. Link didn't think they were just daffy kids. And he even admitted the possibility of a spy in Riverton.

"Tell me all about it," Mr. Link said quietly.

"I found the message," slipped in Shoie, determined to get the credit.

"And Mr. Pinkney is the spy," chimed in the Pest.

But it was Alvin—Secret Agent K-21 1/2—who finally told the entire story. He told it in a rush, not even omitting the fact that he and Shoie were Secret Agents K-21 1/2 and Q-3.

When he had finished, there was a silence in the bright room. Finally, Mr. Link said, "Kids, I hate to disappoint you. You've done a fine job of figuring out exactly what *could* be happening. But it *isn't* happening in Riverton. You see, I know Mr. Pinkney. Matter of fact, he's a close friend of mine. Comes over a couple of times a week to play chess with me."

"He *isn't* a spy?" asked Alvin. "How do you know?"

"Here. Give me the message and I'll show you."

It was then that a terrible thought slipped into the Magnificent Brain. Perhaps Mr. Link was a spy, too!

CHAPTER 3

The Message Is Decoded

ALVIN had been holding the message in his hand. Now he thrust it back into his pocket.

"You're thinking," said Mr. Link slowly, as though he could read minds, "you're thinking that I, too, may be a spy. That I may be helping Mr. Pinkney. Quite possible, of course. But let me assure you that it isn't true."

Mr. Link crossed his hands behind his head, leaned back against the pillow, and began explaining.

"When Herman Pinkney came here three years ago, to establish his business, he was a very lonely man. As you know, he has no family. He has two loves: his garden and chess. Eventually, he asked one of his employees if there were any good chess players in town. He was given my name. That night, Mr. Pinkney appeared on my doorstep.

"We soon became close friends. He is a fine person,

and you kids should get to know him better, for he is a lonely person, as I said. Herman Pinkney has been coming here two, sometimes three night a week to play chess. To me—a lonely man confined to his bed, with only his books to keep him company—such a friendship means a great deal. Frequently, we talk deep into the night about everything from the chess masters to the great works of literature.

"One night Herman told me of a problem he had in connection with his business. As you know, his little factory makes transistor radios, intercoms, and that sort of thing. He sells them all over the world. He must compete not only with the European manufacturers, but also with some fine products from Japan.

"Anyway, this was Herman's problem: At least once a week he had to send instructions to his distributors in Europe. He sent the messages by transatlantic cable, and the cable bills were so high they were cutting into his profits. Furthermore, he had the feeling that a business spy either was working in one of his foreign offices or was intercepting his cables. If a competitor could learn his bid for certain radio parts, Herman could lose a fortune overnight.

"Business codes are not unusual, and because of my experience in code work, I suggested that he use a code, both to protect his business secrets and to save money on his cable bills. What you are holding in your hand, Alvin, is a message from Herman to one of his European distributors."

Alvin stared at the paper in disbelief. "But it says right here, 'Ivan hiding message oak.' That doesn't say anything about business. Sounds like a Russian spy message to me."

Mr. Link pointed to a particular shelf on one wall. "Shoie, you'll find a black notebook over there. Will you bring it to me, please?"

Shoie handed him the notebook.

"Here, Alvin, is the codebook I developed for Herman Pinkney. It enables him to do two things: to protect the secrets of his business, and to save a great deal of money on cablegrams." He handed the book to Alvin. "I want you to look through it, K-21 1/2. You'll find that it contains a list of words and phrases in alphabetical order—quite a long list of business words and phrases. Opposite each entry on this list is a code word which stands for the same thing."

Alvin thumbed through the book. The first page was labeled A and started with the phrase "additional parts arriving soon." In a column just opposite was the word "sofa." The rest of the book was filled with hundreds of business phrases and their corresponding code words.

"This is a good example of a business code," said Mr. Link, "and thousands of businesses all over the world use such codes." From the bedside table, he picked up a pencil and a pad of paper and tossed them to Alvin. "Now, Alvin, write down the message on that scrap of paper in a single column of words, then look

up the meanings of those words in the back of the
code book and write them down."

Alvin did as he was instructed:

SERIOUS	Seven thousand
MILLY	spare parts
HIDING	arriving by plane
THURSDAY	Thursday.
START	Seal them in warehouse
SECRETS	await (awaiting) further instructions
IVAN	George Malloy
HIDING	arriving by plane
MESSAGE	next week
OAK	Frankfurt.
REMAIN	Keep me informed
SILENT	trouble with distributors.
HERMAN	Herman Pinkney

Alvin sat there with the pad of paper in his hand,
staring at it dumfounded. "But—but," he sputtered,
"but I was so sure about Mr. Pinkney, and he has an
oak tree in his back yard, and he doesn't seem very
friendly, and . . ."

"Were you ever very friendly to him?" asked Mr.
Link.

"No," said the Pest promptly. "No, we weren't."

"Then," said Mr. Link softly, "I think we all might
learn a lesson here. A couple of lessons, in fact. The
first is that we should never accept the bad about
someone—only the good—until we know them well.
And the second lesson, Alvin"—he looked straight at

Alvin, somehow sensing K-21 1/2's high interest in the code book—"concerns codes. A man named Arthur Colton once put it very nicely; you'll find it in a book on the shelf over there. Colton said, 'Nothing more completely baffles one who is full of tricks and duplicity than straightforward and simple integrity in another.' That simply means that the easiest way to fool a suspicious person is to be completely honest."

"I get the point," said Alvin, a blush of shame rising on his face.

"Now," said Mr. Link gently, "you kids seem mighty interested in codes. Would you like to learn more about them?"

"Would we!" said Q-3 and K-21 1/2 in unison.

"Me too," piped the Pest.

"All right, let's learn one or two more things from Herman Pinkney's message. First, the code was set up not only to protect business secrets, but to save Herman money. Each word that he sends by cable costs a great deal. Now count the words in his original message."

Alvin carefully counted the words in the right-hand column, tapping his pencil against the paper for each word. "Thirty-one," he announced.

"Now count the words in the coded message: the words he actually paid for."

Alvin paused. "Thirteen."

"Gosh," said Shoie, "in code, the message lost him mess than half, I mean cost him less than half what it would have cost otherwise."

"So I'd say this was a successful code," said Mr. Link. "There have been a good many other codes throughout history that have been suprisingly success-ful—and some dismal flops. A code, or more often a cipher, is simply a message written in such a way that only certain people know how to read it." He reached up to the Pest's golden curls. "Lean over here a minute, and I'll see if *you're* carrying a secret message."

"What?" stammered the Pest, showing the top of her head to Mr. Link.

Gently, he parted her fine hair, looking at the skin on top of her head. "Nope, no secret messages. I do see a scar, though."

"That's from falling off the roof of Maldowski's hen house and landing on my head on a wheelbarrow," the Pest said, somewhat proudly. "We were throwing rot-ten apples down at Gooey Larson. Took ten stitches."

Alvin was puzzled. "Why did you expect to find a secret message on top of the Pest's head?"

"I'm kidding, of course. I just used the Pest's head to illustrate how the ancient Greeks used to send se-cret messages over hundreds of miles. The man send-ing the message would shave the head of one of his slaves. Then he would write the secret message on top of the man's head, and send him on his way. By the time the slave was traveling through enemy territory, his hair would have grown long enough to hide the message. When he arrived at the other end, the receiver of the message would simply shave the slave's head again and read the secret."

"Wait until I get you home with the scissors," said Alvin, kidding the Pest.

She stuck out her tongue at him. "I have a code in my head!" she said.

"Owww!" groaned Shoie. "That's a terrible joke!"

Mr. Link's deep laugh boomed through the room, and he patted the Pest's head.

But Alvin didn't want the discussion of codes to be interrupted. "Go on, Mr. Link. Please tell us more."

CHAPTER 4

Secret Agents, Secret Codes

"ALL RIGHT," said Mr. Link. "Let's figure out, first of all, who might use codes. I think you'll be surprised at the number of people who make use of codes. Anyone have any ideas?"

"The Army and the Navy and the Air Force," said Shoie.

"Diplomats and spies," said Alvin.

"Mr. Pinkney," said the Pest.

"Right," said Mr. Link, with a smile. "Can you think of any others?"

There was a long silence.

"Codes are much more widely used than you would imagine. Do you remember all the letters and numbers on railroad cars? They are code symbols, though not necessarily secret, telling railroad men a great deal about that car and what is inside. I'll give you another example of a business code. Pest, take off your shoe for a minute."

With a slightly baffled expression, the Pest took off her shoe.

"Do you see any numbers inside?" asked Mr. Link.

"Yep. It says 52243, then 63, then 8, then 3135. Is that a code?"

"Certainly is. I can't solve that code, but I can make some guesses. The first batch of numbers—52243— probably represents the particular factory and the machine in the factory that turned out those shoes you're wearing. Then comes 63. I'm almost sure it represents 1963, the year the shoes were made. The 8 means they were made in August, the eighth month. And I'm sure that you wear size 13 1/2C, because 3135 is a universal code among shoemen.

"The first number—3—is the width C, the third letter of the alphabet. If the Pest were wearing a B width, the number would be 2. The middle number or numbers, is the size, 13. And the 5 after the 13 adds the half-size. An 0 means that it *isn't* a half-size. So the Pest wears a 13 1/2C shoe. Now, suppose she had worn a size 7B. What would the code number have been?"

It irritated Alvin that his sister frequently could think faster than the Magnificent Brain. "270," she shouted.

"Right," said Mr. Link.

By now, Shoie was pulling off his own oversized shoes and checking the numbers inside. "It works!" he said, in a somewhat surprised voice. "The size number in here is 495 and I wear a 9 1/2D shoe."

"Do any other businesses use codes?" asked Alvin.

"Most of them do. Take a look at the price tag on almost any item in a department store. In addition to the price, which the owner wants you to know, you'll almost always find a batch of other letters and numbers that don't mean a thing to you. They tell the store owner a great deal, though. They tell him when the shipment arrived, when the item was made, how long it has been in stock, and a good many other things. If you study those tags, you frequently can break the code."

"Tell us more about the messengers with the shaved heads," said the Pest. "I liked that."

Mr. Link smiled. "Suppose I show you how to make a scytale instead. Then you can send your own secret messages."

"What's a scytale?" asked Alvin.

"It's a simple method of sending a coded message, developed hundreds of years before the birth of Christ. You'll find a pair of scytales on that shelf over there, Shoie, the second shelf from the bottom. Bring them over, please."

Shoie looked on the shelf. "Nothing here except books and a couple pieces of wood sawed off an old broom handle. No scytales here."

"Those pieces of wood *are* the scytales. Matter of fact, they *were* sawed off an old broom handle."

Shoie examined them carefully. Each scytale was about a foot long. "Do you mean to say there's a secment compartret, I mean a secret compartment in these things? It certainly doesn't show."

"There's no secret compartment *inside* the scytale. But there's one on the *outside*, for sending secret messages."

"I don't get it," said Alvin.

"On the same shelf, Shoie, you'll find a little roll of paper that I keep on hand to show visitors how a scytale works. Bring it over and we'll send a secret message."

Shoie handed over the two scytales and the little roll of paper. Mr. Link unrolled the paper into a long ribbon, about half an inch wide.

"There's nothing special about the paper," he said. "You can use any paper cut into long strips about this wide." Reaching over to the bedside table, he picked up a roll of tape and taped one end of the ribbon of paper close to the end of one of the scytales. Then, very carefully, he wound the paper around the scytale in a spiral. Each time he turned the scytale, he made sure that the edge of the paper came exactly to the edge of the previous turn. When the paper almost covered the scytale, he tore off the ribbon and taped the end.

"Now, K-21 1/2, let's pretend you want to send a secret message to Q-3. You're going to use the Pest to deliver the message, but you're afraid she'll be caught by the enemy. Take that sheet of paper, there, and write down any message you want to send."

Alvin stuck the tip of the pencil in his mouth, as he usually did when the Magnificent Brain was struggling with a problem. Finally, he wrote, "Enemy agent planning to let air out of your rear bicycle tire. Take precautions. K-21 1/2." He handed the message to Mr. Link.

Mr. Link took the pencil from Alvin and copied the words on the scytale. He wrote one letter on each turn of the paper for the full length of the scytale, then turned the scytale a bit in his hand and made another row of letters, until he had copied the entire message. He was very careful to keep the letters in a straight line across, and he used only large capital letters. Holding the scytale so Shoie couldn't see it, he showed the message to Alvin. "Is your message copied correctly, K-21 1/2?"

"Roger. But if the Pest carries that stick, anyone can read the message."

Mr. Link unstuck the tape at one end, and pulled the paper carelessly off the wooden rod. He rolled it into a small cylinder and handed it to the Pest. "Our lives may depend upon you delivering this secretly and safely," he said in a solemn voice. "Our hearts and prayers go with you."

The Pest was bewildered. "You want me to hand this to Shoie, across the room?"

"Right. But first we'll pretend that Alvin here, instead of sending the message, now is an enemy counterspy. He has captured you and tortured you until you hand over the message. Now give it to this terrible, terrible counterspy."

Reluctantly, the Pest handed the little roll of paper to Alvin.

"Read the message," said Mr. Link, "so you'll know what Agent K-21 1/2 is planning."

Alvin unrolled the message. A look of bewilderment crossed his face.

"Read the message," repeated Mr. Link.

"I can't. It's just a batch of jumbled-up letters."

"Your secret message is still secret, even though it's in the hands of an enemy agent?"

"Right."

"Now let's pretend that the Pest hasn't been caught, but can still deliver the message. Pest, deliver the message to Agent Q-3."

As usual, the Pest dramatized her role. By the time she handed over the message to Shoie, she was on her hands and knees gasping for breath.

Mr. Link tossed Shoie the other wooden rod. "Now, Q-3, you have in your possession a rod exactly like Alvin's. Wind up the message on your scytale in the same way I did originally."

Shoie carefully wound the paper around the piece of broom handle. Then he turned the scytale slowly in his hands. A grin broke across his face. "You're kidding, aren't you, Alvin? Nobody's really letting the air out of my ticycle bires?"

"Wow," said Alvin. "I'm going to make a scytale as soon as I get home."

"All you need is an old broomstick. The only thing to remember is that the sender and the receiver of the message must each have a scytale *exactly* the same diameter. The length doesn't make any difference, but they must be exactly the same distance around, and the message must be wound neatly or the letters will be scrambled."

Alvin suddenly had a faraway look in his eye. The Magnificent Brain had locked onto a problem. "All the letters in my message to Shoie are on that piece of paper, but they're scrambled up. Mr. Pinkney's code didn't even use the same letters. How many different kinds of codes are there?"

"Zillions. So many you couldn't even count them. There's a difference between a code and a cipher. A *code* is what Mr. Pinkney uses. One word—any word he selects, or even a made-up word such as MELUG—stands for a *thought*. In order to use a *code*, you have to think of every possible message you'll ever want to send, and work out code words to explain those thoughts."

"I could make up some good words," said the Pest. "Like magniflorospound and kratchnee."

"I imagine you could. Then you have to write down all those words and their meanings in two books, one for the sender and the other for the receiver. You can't possibly remember all those words and their meanings.

So there are at least two code books in existence, which may be captured by the enemy. The captain of each ship in the Navy has such a code book. The book is covered with sheets of lead, so it is very heavy. If his ship is in danger of being sunk or captured, the captain's first duty is to drop the book over the side, where it will sink to the depths of the ocean and be lost forever."

Alvin was still puzzled. "Then a code has one word that stands for several other words. What's a cipher?"

"A cipher is simply an alphabet, though it may be a very strange one. You give each letter of the alphabet some corresponding sign, number, or letter. If you wanted to invent a simple cipher, for example, you could decide that in writing out the letters of the message you'd use the *second following letter* of the alphabet. Then each time you wanted to use the letter A, you'd use C instead. In this case, your name, Alvin, would be C-N-X-K-P."

"Hello, Snickskup," said the Pest, running the letters together.

"Do you see any advantages—or disadvantages—to a cipher?"

"You don't need a code book," said Shoie, "as long as you both know the system. You don't have to worry about the enemy stealing your code book."

"Right. The secret of many ciphers can be kept right in your head. Any other advantages?"

"You can send *any* message," said Alvin, "even

though you didn't remember to put it in the code book. You can send any message because you can use every letter of the alphabet."

"Right again. But there's one disadvantage to a cipher. No matter how puzzling your cipher may appear to be, it is easier to break than a code, because all you're doing is rearranging the letters of the alphabet—or symbols for them—in a new way."

"I'll bet I could invent a cipher nobody could break," boasted Alvin.

"And I'll bet you can't," said Mr. Link. "I'll tell you what you do, Alvin. You invent your own cipher, and write a message in it. If it is at least fifty words long, I'll bet I can break it."

The Magnificent Brain started dreaming of strange figures. "Might take a day or two," he hedged.

"Teach us how to break codes *now*," begged the Pest.

"Well, the first thing is . . ."

Just then Mrs. Murphy appeared in the doorway. "Can you children stay for lunch? It's been a long time since I cooked for three young appetites."

Alvin looked at his watch. "Wow! We'd better run. It's twelve-thirty. Thanks for the invitation, but we've got to go."

"Some other time then," said Mrs. Murphy.

"Oh, we'd like to come back. Maybe tomorrow afternoon? And when we come, I'll bring a secret message in a cipher that even Mr. Link won't be able to break."

On the way home they saw Mr. Pinkney mounding dirt around his roses for the winter.

Alvin thought for a moment, then waved his hand and shouted, "Hi, Mr. Pinkney!"

Startled, the man looked up. "Well, hi," he called back. "Hi, kids!" A broad grin broke across his face.

CHAPTER 5

Tale of a Buried Treasure

IMMEDIATELY after lunch Alvin and Shoie headed for the basement to make a pair of scytales. Mrs. Fernald had already gone downtown to do some shopping. It was Sergeant Fernald's day off, and he'd settled into his easy chair to watch the ball game on TV. The Pest was doing the dishes.

On the way to the basement, Alvin passed the broom closet and looked inside. A mop was hanging there, with a perfectly good handle. He told himself that his mother would never use the mop again, that the mop was too old, and that it was worn out. Finally, he talked himself into taking it to the basement.

The mop handle was in the vise and had already been sawed in half when Alvin heard his dad's footsteps on the stairs. He hurriedly took the mop out of the vise and tossed it into a dark corner behind the bench. The Pest came bouncing down the steps behind her father.

44

"Hi, Shoie," said Sergeant Fernald. "What are you two cooking up down here?" Alvin's father, a very neat, precise man, was always interested in what his children were doing, but never interfered unless he saw that some kind of damage would result. That was quite often.

"Hi, Mr. Fernald," said Shoie. "We weren't doing much. Just starting to make a couple of scytales."

"Scy-what?"

"Scytales. They're for sending messages in secret code. Alvin and I are Secret Agents and . . ."

"We'll show you when we're through, Dad," said Alvin. His thoughts were on the mop in the corner.

"Alvin, I wish you and Shoie would do me a favor this afternoon. Next Tuesday is your mother's wedding anniversary—*our* wedding anniversary—and I want to get her a gift, something we'll all enjoy. Several months ago she mentioned how nice it would be if we could afford a stereo hi-fi set."

"Stereo hi-fi set," repeated the Pest. "Oh, Daddy, are we *really* going to get one?"

"That depends. Last week your mother and I were passing Billings' Department Store. In the window was a hi-fi set that just matches our furniture. I could see that she liked it, so we went inside and priced it. It's about fifty dollars more than we can afford to spend right now. Mr. Billings showed us some other hi-fi's, but said they weren't the same quality as the one in the window. Frankly, I don't know anything about the amplifiers and speakers in those things, not even as much as you do, Alvin. I wish you and Shoie would go down to Billings' and check the set. Take a look at some of the others, too, and let me know what you think."

"Sure, Dad." Alvin always liked to be asked his professional opinion.

As his father turned to go up the stairs, he said, almost to himself, "I certainly wish we could afford that set in the window, but I'm afraid it's just too expensive."

"Can I come with you, Alvin?" asked the Pest.

"What do you know about power outputs and ohms and —and watts, and all that kind of stuff?" said Alvin. He didn't know much either, but he pretended he did. "Come on, Shoie. We'll go down to Billings' right now. We can make the scytales later."

On the way upstairs, his father said, "I don't particularly like to do business with Mr. Billings— he's just a little too sharp in the way he operates—but your mother likes that particular set. Maybe we can find another set somewhere else that doesn't cost as much."

Alvin was putting on his jacket when the doorbell rang. "I'll get it," he called to his Dad, who had gone back to the ball game.

He opened the front door. A woman about his mother's age stood there. She had a pleasant, friendly face, with crinkles at the corners of her eyes, as though she laughed a lot. In her hair was just a touch of gray.

"Hello, there," she said. "Is Sergeant Fernald home?"

"Yes, he's here. Would you like to come in?" He held the door open for her and called, "Dad, there's someone here to see you."

Sergeant Fernald appeared in the hallway. "How do you do?" he said. "I'm Sergeant Fernald."

"I'm Miss Alicia Fenwick." Her voice was soft. "I've driven up here from Mississippi, and I would very much appreciate it if you would give me just a few minutes of your time."

"Of course. Won't you come in and sit down?"

Alvin said, "We'll go on down to Billings', Dad."

Miss Fenwick smiled at him. "Please don't leave because I arrived. As a matter of fact, perhaps you children can help me, too." She spoke with the soft tones that Alvin could remember so well from the vacation trip they'd taken through the South. "Besides, what I have to discuss with your father has a lot of adventure, danger, excitement—and a little blood in it. Just the sort of a story you might enjoy."

Dad said, "If there's any possibility that you kids can help Miss Fenwick, hang around for a few minutes. You can go downtown later."

In the living room he switched off the TV and introduced the kids to Miss Fenwick. Alvin liked her immensely, for some reason he could not quite understand. He could tell that the Pest did too, because she chose to sit on the footstool in front of Miss Fenwick's chair.

"Now, how can we be of help?" asked Sergeant Fernald.

"Perhaps I should tell you first that I have children, too." She reached out and ran her fingers lightly through the Pest's golden curls. "Forty-two children, to be exact."

"Wow!" said Shoie. "You're not that old. Unless you've had a lot of trins and twiplets. I mean, I mean, that must be some kind of a record, or ..." His voice stopped abruptly in confusion.

"They're not really my children, of course." She smiled. "Though I like to think they are. You see, I run an orphanage. It was started by my parents when I was a small child. It really started with one little boy who was all alone in the world. That boy is now a United States Senator." She said it proudly. "Since then, 465 children have been helped by our orphanage, without a penny from any state, local, or national government."

"It sounds most worthwhile," said Dad. "But we have our own charities here, to which we contribute."

Miss Fenwick held up her hand. "Please don't misunderstand me. I'm not here asking for money for the orphanage —though we badly need it. I'm here to find someone, a mysterious Mr. Smith. I doubt if that's his real name, but they told me at the police station that you might be of help in finding him, because you know everyone in Riverton."

"What's this man Smith's first name?"

"I don't know. He simply signed his name J. A. Smith. He wrote me one note, with no return address, and it was mailed from Riverton."

"What did he want?"

"In order to tell you that, I must tell you a longer story which goes back into history a bit." She looked at the children. "And that's where the mystery comes in. It may take fifteen minutes to tell this mystery story. Can you children wait that long?"

"If it's a mystery," said Alvin. "We like mystery stories."

"In a way it *is* a mystery story, and it started during the Civil War. My great-great-grandfather, Elijah Fenwick, was one of the wealthiest planters of the South. He had a huge cotton plantation. During the war, all the men—even boys almost as young as you boys—left that part of the country to fight. Only my great-great-grandfather, who was almost eighty years old, was left at home with the slaves."

"I don't like that part about the slaves," said the Pest.

"Neither do I, honey. Slavery was a terrible thing, but in those days, it was accepted throughout the South. And as far as I can find out, Elijah Fenwick was very kind to his slaves. Anyway, with all the men away at war, the bushwhackers moved in."

"What's a bushwhacker?" asked Alvin.

"The bushwhackers were simply packs of bandits—

most of them deserters from one of the two armies. Some were criminals who had been released from Southern prisons in the hope they would fight for the South, but who simply deserted and began stealing.

"The bushwhackers hid in the forests and swamps of our area of the South. Whenever they needed food, money, or anything else, they came riding out to one of the plantations, killed anyone who resisted, and took everything of value. Because all the men had gone to war, there was no one to stop them.

"It was toward the end of the war that bushwhackers first appeared in the area right around my family's plantation. Elijah Fenwick was afraid that they would soon come riding up to his home and steal everything of value."

"Why didn't he hide his stuff?" asked Shoie.

"That's exactly what he did. And he did it with the help of a remarkable man who had been one of his slaves.

"The man's name was Adam Moses, but he was simply called Mr. Moses by everyone who knew him. He had grown up on the plantation, and, as a child, he had been so appealing and intelligent that Elijah Fenwick had taught him to read and write. Mr. Moses grew into a very fine, very wise man, known and loved by my family as well as by his own people. Eventually, he became supervisor of all the slaves on the plantation. And not long before the war broke out, Elijah Fenwick had freed him."

"Good for him," said the Pest.

"It was to Mr. Moses that Elijah turned for help when all his possessions were in danger. One night, long after everyone else had gone to sleep, they crept through the house, assembling everything of any great value. This included the family silver, all the money on the plantation, the jewelry— everything that could be packed into a small iron-bound chest. When they had finished, it was a genuine treasure chest. No one knows what it would be worth today, but my guess is around a quarter of a million dollars."

"Wow!" said Alvin.

Shoie whistled.

The Pest leaned so far forward that she fell off the footstool. "Then what happened?" she asked, her eyes shining.

"The old man and Mr. Moses, late on that moon-less night, carried the chest out of the house. They buried it in one of the flower beds, replaced the soil carefully, and even replanted the flowers exactly as they were before. I know all this because my great-grandfa-ther told me the story when I was a little girl."

"Did the bushwhackers ever come?" asked Alvin.

"Yes, they came riding out of the woods three days later. They made Elijah Fenwick lead them to all the food on the plantation. Then they tied him in the veg-etable cellar. He could hear a great deal of shouting and crying from outside, but there was nothing he could do. It was late that night before any of the slaves had the courage to creep down into the cellar and free him.

"When he came out into the night air, the first thing he did was check on the safety of all his people, slaves and family alike. Some had been mistreated and a few slaves had run off, but no one was badly hurt. The second thing he did was to check the flower bed where the treasure had been buried. All he found was a deep hole, with the flowers trampled all around. The treasure had disappeared with the bushwhackers." Miss Fenwick paused. "And so had Mr. Moses and his little son."

"Was the treasure ever found?" asked Sergeant Fernald. He was leaning forward, puffing his pipe.

"That comes at the end of my story. Within a few months the war ended. Of course, the slaves were freed, but most of them stayed with my family. It was a terrible time. There was very little food, and with the treasure gone, there was no money. But I think the biggest blow to Elijah Fenwick was not the loss of his lifetime possessions but the fact that Mr. Moses, whom he had trusted, had disappeared, along with his little son Adam.

"Then, months later, a letter arrived. At that time my own grandfather, Elijah Fenwick's grandson, was a boy about your age, Alvin. He watched his grandfather seated on the front steps of the old plantation house, open the envelope with trembling hands. His hands were shaking because he recognized Mr. Moses's handwriting on the envelope. As he read the letter, the tears streamed down his face."

Miss Fenwick reached into her purse. Carefully, she drew out a yellowed and tattered piece of paper and, very slowly, so as not to damage it, she unfolded it. She turned to Alvin's father. "Here is that letter from Mr. Moses. I'd like you to read it."

"Read it aloud, Dad!" said Alvin excitedly.

Dad carefully took out his glasses, put them on, and looked over the tattered paper. Then he started to read:

"Dear Master Elijah,

"I am writing this by firelight at night somewhere in Indiana. I am afraid for my life, but I am even more afraid that you will never forgive me, after you have done so much for me.

"I shall never forget that terrible day. After the men tied you in the vegetable cellar, they rounded up all of my people and held them at gunpoint while they searched the house. A big bearded man appeared to be the leader, a man they called Blacky. I have since learned that his real name is Blackwell. He had been a spy in the Union Army, but he deserted and became leader of that band of evil men.

"When he found there was nothing of value in the house, he was in a terrible rage. He slapped some of the womenfolk around and told them to point to the man who would know where the money was hidden. I am proud that not one of them told him the secret, but

I suppose he could tell from the way they looked toward me that I was the man who might know. My son Adam was holding onto me, and Blacky locked everyone in the barn but the two of us.

"He beat me, but I did not speak a word that might tell him where we had buried the chest. Finally, he held young Adam by his little neck and threatened to squeeze the life right out of him if I did not tell. Master Elijah, I couldn't stand to see my boy's eyes pop out. I told him where the chest was buried, the Lord forgive me. And may you forgive me, too.

"They made me dig up the chest, and load it on the old mule we call Jake. I was afraid they were going to kill me on the spot, but they took me along to work for them. When I led old Jake away from home, it was the saddest day of my life. I hope my son has recovered from that terrible time.

"They took me with them to live on the island in the middle of Miller's Swamp. I couldn't get away. They worked me hard each day, and at night they chained me to a tree.

"Finally, we heard that the war was over and that the menfolk, praise the Lord, were coming home. Blacky said that after the way his men had stolen everything for scores of miles around, they'd better head North in a hurry.

"I had to lead old Jake along the back trails, loaded down with your chest, Master Elijah. After about a week, old Jake gave out, and they shot him right there.

I cried when it happened. He was the best mule I ever saw. Do you remember how he used to tear into those cotton fields?

"We loaded the chest on a spare horse and kept moving. The men stopped just long enough to take food from the poor families along the road. Finally, after we had traveled for months, a Yankee army unit started after us. I reckon they had heard of all we'd done along the way. By then we were up here in Indiana somewhere, I don't know just where.

"The Yankees attacked Blacky and his men one rainy morning. We could see them coming, off across the fields. Just as soon as the firing started, I felt cold metal on the back of my neck. I knew it was a gun even before I looked around. Blacky whispered to me to sneak back with him to where the horses were tied in a willow grove.

"By the time we got to the horses, the firing was fierce, and I reckon the rest of the men didn't even know we had skedaddled. Blacky kept that big gun pointed at me and made me ride ahead of him, leading the pack horse that carried your chest, Master.

"After maybe ten miles we came to some rough country, where a river ran between some bluffs, and the pack horse began to founder. I wish I could tell you exactly where it was.

"Blacky shouted to me to stop and made me dig a deep hole with a flat piece of stone. I dug the hole between two boulders. Then he had me put your chest in the hole and bury it and cover the fresh dirt with loose rocks.

"When I had finished the work, he aimed that big pistol at me and said, 'Ain't going to be anybody but me around who knows where that treasure is buried.' I knew right then that my time had come. I still had a rock in my hand and the Lord must have helped me aim, because it hit the wrist that was holding the pistol. I ran for one of the horses and rode away from there in a hurry.

"Once, from the top of the bluffs, I looked down and saw him pacing off the ground between some rocks. I reckon he was figuring how to find the treasure again. He saw me looking down on him and shook his fist at me.

"Now I know he's tracking me, because I'm the only other man who knows where your chest is buried. Yesterday I saw him a long way across the fields.

"Lord help me reach you, Master Elijah, so I can beg your forgiveness. I think I could find your treasure again, as I've been remembering the country I passed through.

"My horse is about tuckered out and so am I. If I pass a farm tomorrow, I'll ask them to see that this letter reaches you. I can't stay with them though, as Blacky might harm such folk. Now I must start out again through the darkness, for I feel that he will soon be here.

"God bless you, Master Elijah. If you receive this

letter, I beg you to take care of my family. And I beg
your forgiveness, just as I beg the forgiveness of the
good Lord every hour of the day.

Mr. Moses"

There was a long silence after Sergeant Fernald had
finished the letter. Finally, he cleared his throat and
looked up at Miss Fenwick. "Did you ever hear what
happened to Mr. Moses?"

"Yes. Within an hour of reading the letter, Elijah
Fenwick sent a man North to try to find Mr. Moses.
He returned three months later. He had finally learned
what had happened. The Yankee army had found Mr.
Moses, within three miles of what is now Riverton, In-
diana, with his throat cut."

"Gosh!" said Alvin. It came out like the croak of a
frog. He cleared his throat. "How about Blacky? Does
anyone know what happened to him?"

"Yes. The Army trailed him to the home of a relative. He resisted and was killed inside the house."

"Was the treasure ever found?" asked Shoie.

"No. Not as far as I can find out. Apparently the secret of the spot where the treasure is buried died with
Mr. Moses and Blacky."

No one spoke for a full minute, and Alvin could
hear the ticking of the old clock on the mantel. Finally,
he asked,

"What happened to Mr. Moses' little boy?"

"He had been so terrified by Blacky that he'd run

away. A good-hearted family that lived about fifty
miles north found him hiding along the river, a lost
and silent little child. The shock of what had happened to him had been so great that he couldn't make
a sound. They took him into their home and treated
him well. Finally one morning, months later, his voice
returned as suddenly as it had vanished, and he told
them everything that had happened. They returned
him to the Fenwick plantation."

Sergeant Fernald cleared his throat. "And that story
brings you here just now, Miss Fenwick? Why?"

"About two months ago I received a strange letter."
Miss Fenwick again opened her purse and brought
forth an envelope. "There's no return address. Just a
Riverton postmark. This is all the letter says: 'If you
have any papers concerning the Fenwick treasure,
write me at the following address: J. A. Smith, General
Delivery, Riverton, Indiana.' There's not even a signature on it."

"Where's General Delivery?" asked the Pest. "We
have a General MacArthur Street in Riverton, but I
don't remember any General Delivery Street."

Sergeant Fernald smiled. "General Delivery simply
means the post office, honey. All you have to do is go
into the post office and ask for any mail addressed to
you."

"I guess that's what Mr. Smith did," said Miss
Fenwick in her soft voice. "I wrote a long reply, telling
the story of the treasure just as I've told it to you. I

even sent a copy of Mr. Moses' letter. I asked Mr. J. A. Smith to contact me immediately, but I've never heard a word from him."

Sergeant Fernald walked over to the table and re-filled his pipe. "My guess is that Mr. J. A. Smith is not that letter writer's real name. I think someone knows of the existence of the treasure and simply wanted to learn whether you had any information that might be useful in finding it. There's not much information along that line in Mr. Moses's letter, so Mr J. A. Smith—or whatever his name is—has decided that he'd better not stir your interest in this any further."

"Oh, but I am interested," she said. "Is there any way you can help me find the man? I'm so interested that I came here on my vacation, instead of going West as I'd planned. If there's the slightest chance the treasure will be discovered, I want to be here."

She gazed at a corner of the room for a moment. Then she said softly and slowly, "I figure that the trea-sure is still the property of the Fenwick family. And I'm all that's left of the Fenwick family. Oh, I don't want it for myself. I want it for the orphanage. We're almost out of money and I don't know which way to turn. If we don't get more money soon, I'll have to start turning away children."

Sergeant Fernald cleared his throat. "There are half-a-dozen families named Smith in Riverton, but none with the initials J. A. I know all of these families pretty well, and I don't believe there's anyone that would be writing you a letter about the treasure. How long will you be in town, Miss Fenwick?"

"I can stay a week or more, if it will be of any help."

Sergeant Fernald lighted his pipe. "I don't like to discourage you, but I can't honestly see much you can do. However, Harvey Mills, who tends the window over at the post office, might remember something about the man who picked up your reply. Harvey's probably gone fishing for the weekend, so I doubt if we'll be able to see him until Monday."

"I'd appreciate it very much if you'd visit Mr. Mills with me on Monday." She smiled and stood up. "Now I really have taken up too much of your time, Sergeant Fernald. But there's one last question I'd like to ask before I go to my hotel." She seemed a bit embarrassed. "Perhaps it's silly of me even to ask, but have you ever heard any stories of buried treasure around here?"

There was a long silence. Then Alvin leaped to his feet, smacking the heel of his hand against the Magnificent Brain. "I know something," he said excitedly. "Remember the river bluffs southwest of town? The ones they're talking about turning into a state park?"

Shoie and the Pest jumped up at the same time.

"I got your wave thoughts, old bean!" shouted Shoie.

"Me, too!" said the Pest.

"What's all this about?" asked Sergeant Fernald.

"Don't you remember?" said Alvin. "Everybody calls them the river bluffs now. But several years ago, when

I was the Pest's age"—he stood up a little taller—
"most everybody called them Treasure Bluffs."

"That's true," said Sergeant Fernald.

"And when we were kids"—Alvin always liked to
talk like a grown-up in front of grown-ups—"everybody said there was a secret treasure buried in the
bluffs."

"Everybody? Who's everybody?"

"Why, all the other kids."

"And where did they hear it?"

"From the other kids, I suppose."

"I'm afraid that's not much good," said Dad. "Even
if there *is* a treasure buried there, you can't just go out
and start digging. You have to know where to dig."

"Well," said Alvin, "we could at least look around."

"I'm sure you won't find it just lying there, ready to
be picked up," said the Sergeant. "However, Miss
Fenwick might like to see the bluffs. I'll take her out
there for a ride when your mother comes back."

"Can we come?" begged Alvin.

"No," said his father, with finality. "You really must
go on that errand downtown, if we are going to get
your mother an anniversary gift by Tuesday."

"Darn it," said Alvin.

"Darn it," echoed the Pest.

Dad turned to Miss Fenwick. "I hope, somehow, we
can be of help in solving this mystery."

"I hope so, too. If I don't succeed, we'll not only
have to turn away children from the orphanage, but

start cutting down the staff." She paused. Then she added in a voice almost too low to hear, "The staff consists of five great-grandchildren of Adam Moses."

CHAPTER 6

Money from a Broken Code

THE THREE kids stood in front of the window of Billings' Department Store.

"Gosh, isn't it a beauty?" There was awe in the Pest's voice.

Indeed it was a beauty—a high-styled hi-fi set, rubbed to a soft glow, in a natural wood finish that just matched their furniture.

"I can see why Mom wants it," said Alvin, "but look at the sign."

A big sign behind the set read, "JUST ARRIVED. THE VERY LATEST IN STEREO SETS. WHY BE SATISFIED WITH YOUR OLD SET? ONLY $215."

"Wow!" said Shoie. "That's a lot of money!"

"Let's go inside." Alvin led the way through the revolving door.

Inside, the store was busy with Saturday shoppers. Alvin led the way past the washing machines, ranges, TV sets, and sewing machines, until they stood in the hi-fi section looking at the various sets on display.

"There's nothing here halfway as good-looking as the one in the window," said the Pest.

Alvin was inclined to agree, but tried to put on an air of knowledge. "It isn't the appearance that counts; it's the sound. Look, there's another just like the one in the window."

They walked over and huddled around it. Just then, Mr. Billings bustled up, frowning. He was a stout little man, who continually washed his hands in the air. At least, that's what it looked like to Alvin.

"You kids will have to leave," said Mr. Billings. "I don't want you breaking any of this valuable equipment, and you're in the way of the customers."

Alvin stood his ground. "My dad sent me down to shop for a hi-fi set. Anything I like, he's going to buy." It was only a *slight* exaggeration.

Mr. Billings' face broke into a smile. "Well, that's different. Say, aren't you Sergeant Fernald's boy? Of course, of course. Your father was in last week looking at hi-fi sets. You children are always welcome in this store. Please look all you'd like."

"We'd like a demonstration," said Alvin.

"Are you sure your father said he'd buy the set you liked?"

Alvin thought for a moment. "He said he's going to

buy a set and for us to pick out a good one."

"Well . . . well." Mr. Billings washed his hands in the air. "By all means, let's have a demonstration." He placed a record on the turntable and warmed up the set that was identical to the one in the window. "This is the very latest thing. Just arrived. Listen to the magnificent sound."

And it *was* magnificent. Every tone as clear as a bell. Alvin could feel the bass notes going right through the soles of his feet.

"Now," said Mr. Billings, "listen to the same record on this one. Of course, it isn't as expensive, so you can't expect the sound to be as good."

To Alvin, there wasn't a great deal of difference, but the Pest had a fine musical ear.

"Oh, it's not nearly as good," she whispered.

Alvin folded his arms and stood there, eyeing the sets critically. "Do you have the specifications in these sets? The amplifier output and the size of the speakers?"

"Of course. It's right there on the price ticket." Mr. Billings spotted another customer looking over a washing machine. "Why don't you kids look around a little? Make yourselves right at home. I'll be back in a minute." He walked away, rubbing his hands.

Alvin looked at the price tag. It included a complete description of the hi-fi. Idly, he noticed a series of numbers at the top of the tag: 5928 3 1860. "Say," he said, "here's what Mr. Link was talking about. It's a secret code."

"I wonder what the numbers mean," said Q-3.

The Pest walked over to another set. "Here's another number. It's different. It says 7312 9 563."

Agent K-21 1/2 went into action, striding from set to set, comparing numbers. Brain clicking like a computer, he sidled up to Q-3. "I think I've solved part of the code," he whispered. "The first four numbers on the tag tell what the set is. Of those four, the first three tell what model it is and the last one is a number for this particular set." He showed Shoie two tags. "See? All sets like this one have the same first three numbers on them. The fourth number is the number of this particular set."

Shoie was impressed. "I think you're right. But that leaves two other batches of numbers on each tag. What do they stand for?"

Studying the tags again, Alvin discovered that the second number in each case was a low one. He found a 4, a 2, a 10, a 6, and an 11.

"Shoie," he directed, "walk around the store and look at the *second* batch of numbers on each tag. Let me know anything you find."

The Pest trailed along with Shoie, while Alvin stood back and let his brain nuzzle the problem around.

Shoie was back within one minute. "Doesn't seem to mean anything," he reported. "The second noup of grumbers, I mean group of numbers on every tag in the store is from 1 to 12. Nothing higher than that."

"What do you mean, it doesn't mean anything?" The excitement of discovery was building up inside Alvin. "No 13s? Nothing higher than 12?"

"Not a 13 in the store."

"We've just broken another part of the code! Can't you see what this means?"

"Can't see a thing except a number."

"Except a number," echoed the Pest.

Alvin tried to be patient. "What goes from 1 to 12, but never on to 13?"

"A dozen eggs?" asked the Pest hopefully.

Alvin was disgusted. "No, no! The months of the year! The months of the year!"

A look of wonder crossed Shoie's face. "You're right," he said. "If it's a 3, it means March. If it's a 4, it means April."

"Right, old bean," said Alvin proudly.

"Oh, Alvin, you're wonderful," said the Pest.

"Now we've got to attack the last group of numbers," said K-21 1/2 with a professional air. "Let's see if we can break the code."

They studied the tag in front of them.

"I have a hunch," said Alvin. "Check the rest of the tags and look at only the last two numbers in the whole code. Just the last two," he repeated.

Three minutes later they were back together in the hi-fi section.

"Report!" ordered K-21 1/2.

"Every tag I looked at," said Shoie, "ended in a 60, a 61, a 62, or a 63. There was only one 60. Most of them were 63s."

"Same here," said the Pest.

"I guess we know what that means," said the top Secret Agent. "That number shows the year each appliance was made. A 63 means it was made in nineteen sixty-three."

"What about the numbers before the 63?" asked the Pest. She looked at a tag on one of the cheaper hi-fi sets. "The last group of numbers on this tag is 2763."

"I think I know the answer to that," said Alvin. "Take a quick look and see if you can find any numbers over 31."

They were back in a moment.

"Nope," said Shoie. "All under 31. And I can guess what that means!"

"The day of the month!" broke in the Pest.

Alvin fumbled through his jacket until he found a stub of a pencil and a scrap of paper. "Watch," he said. Stepping over to the set that his mother wanted, he copied off the code number, then rewrote it, leaving spaces at different intervals:

5928 3 1860

592 8 3 18 60

He looked at it for a moment. "Why, Mr. Billings

isn't completely honest!" he said indignantly. "Look! The 592 is the model number. The 8 is the number of this particular set. And it arrived on March 18, 1960. This set is four years old!"

"You're right, old bean," said Shoie, almost shouting.

"But Mom wants *this* set!" wailed the Pest.

"Of course she does," said Alvin. "And just because it's old doesn't mean it isn't a fine hi-fi set. But the sign in the window says it just arrived and is the very latest set."

Shoie was still lost in the wonders of the code. "Wow! We can decode every tag in this store."

Just then Mr. Billings walked up, a smile on his face. "Well, now," he said. "What nice-looking children!" He patted the Pest on the head. "Always glad to have you children in the store. Have you decided which set to recommend to your father? I hope you recognize what a fine hi-fi this is. Just arrived. I have it right here, ready for delivery Monday or Tuesday."

"Mr. Billings," said Alvin, looking up at him, "this set, which is model number 592 and set number 8, arrived in your store on March 18, 1960. Yet you say in the window that it just arrived and that it's the latest thing out. How do you account for that?"

The hands suddenly stopped their rubbing motion.

"How," sputtered Mr. Billings, "how did you . . ."

"And that sewing machine over there is more than two years old." Alvin purposely raised his voice slightly. "Of course, it has a sign on it that says it's this year's model."

Several customers were beginning to look in their direction. A worried expression crossed Mr. Billings' face. "I think you kids better get out of this store right now."

"All right," said Alvin, raising his voice even higher. "We'll be glad to go. Of course, we can read every tag in the store and make comments on the way out."

"Young man, that's blackmail!"

Alvin looked innocent. He could almost see the thought pass through Mr. Billings' mind, for the hands started rubbing again and a rather sickly smile crossed his face.

"I've been thinking about reducing the price of some of our older hi-fi sets for some time," he said in a low voice. "Do you think your father might be interested in this particular set at a lower price?"

"He might," said Alvin, not giving much ground. "How much do you plan to reduce the price of this old set?"

"Perhaps fif—perhaps seventy-five dollars?" It was a question.

"I think my dad would be very much interested in this set at that price. I'll suggest that he stop in to see you Monday." Alvin looked at Shoie and the Pest. There was a faint light of triumph in his eyes. "Now we must be going. Goodbye, Mr. Billings." Alvin turned and walked out.

They stopped for a moment around the corner in front of the firehouse. Finally, the Pest broke the silence. "Alvin, I think you're wonderful."

Shoie put out his hand. "Great work, old man," he said simply.

"Thanks, old bean."

The three decoders walked down the street, playfully pushing each other.

CHAPTER 7

A Lesson in Cryptography

SUNDAY afternoon Alvin disappeared into his room, energized his burglar alarm, and went to work. Not a sound could be heard from that part of the house for two hours. Twice the Pest tried to get in, and both times the alarm bell sent her scurrying back downstairs.

Finally, in the middle of the afternoon, Shoie arrived, and he and the Pest were allowed to enter. Alvin was sitting at his desk, which was completely covered with balls of crumpled paper that had overflowed and half covered the floor. There was a feverish gleam in Alvin's eye.

"Remind me," he muttered, still working with a pencil and a paper, "to give my brain a rest after this is all over. I've been working it overtime."

"Gosh!" said Shoie. "You look like you've been trying to invent paper snowballs."

"What *have* you been doing, Alvin?" asked the Pest.

"Fooling Mr. Link," said Alvin. He added triumphantly, "And I'll bet I've done it!"

He picked up a sheet of paper from his desk. "You remember that he said he could break any secret code—I mean cipher—that I could invent. Well, here's one he won't break."

"That," said Shoie, "is the wildest piece of paper I ever saw. Looks like a wicken chalked across it, I mean chicken walked across it with muddy feet."

"A chicken with *real* muddy feet," said the Pest. "Do you mean there's a message written there?"

"Sure. Matter of fact, your name's in it, Shoie."

"What does it say?" asked the Pest.

"I'm not going to tell you. You might give parts of it away when Mr. Link tries to break it. And to make it even harder for Mr. Link, I'm going to put it on my scytale."

He searched beneath the pile of papers on his desk until he found the piece of mop handle which he had rescued from the basement that morning. Cutting a sheet of paper into long, narrow strips, he taped them together and wound them carefully on his scytale. Then he copied the symbols onto the scytale, unwound the strip, and looked it over with an air of victory.

"There. He'll *never* be able to read that. Come on. Let's go over there right now. I want to see the look on his face when he sees *this* code."

Mrs. Murphy opened the door with a smile. "He's been talking about you children, hoping you'd be back soon."

To Alvin, Mr. Link looked like a lion, sitting there in bed with his big mop of gray hair flowing around his head like a mane. "Hi, kids," he said cheerfully. "How's the secret agent business?"

"Alvin's the greatest secret agent there is," said the Pest. "Already he's saved Dad seventy-five dollars by breaking a secret code."

Alvin sat back, trying to be modest, while she and Shoie told Mr. Link the story of the hi-fi set. Mr. Link seemed to enjoy it immensely.

"Well I'll be doggoned!" He slapped the thin line that marked his right leg beneath the sheet. "So you solved a secret code, saved your father seventy-five dollars, and got your mother an anniversary gift." He laughed uproariously, shaking his big head from side to side.

"That isn't why we came," said Alvin. "We came to show you the secret code I invented that you can't break. I'll bet nobody can break it."

"Well, let's take a look. Bring it over here."

Alvin handed him the ribbon of paper in triumph.

Mr. Link looked it over. "It's obvious you've used a scytale. There are even ways to break that kind of message. Shoie, will you please hand me the batch of sticks on the bottom shelf over there?"

Shoie produced a dozen wooden rods. Each was a different diameter. Mr. Link began winding the paper ribbon on one, discarded it, and tried another. Finally, he found the one he wanted.

"How do you know which one to use?" asked Shoie.

"You just keep trying different sizes until the symbols line up in nice even lines. Then you know you have a scytale of just the right diameter."

On a sheet of paper, he carefully copied off the weird symbols. Alvin could see that the sheet looked just like his message before he'd rewritten it on the scytale.

For long moments Mr. Link studied the marks on the paper. Then he picked up a pencil and a big pad of paper from the table beside the bed.

"It's a good code, Alvin, but if you kids want to gather around the bed here, where you can watch, I think I can break this code and read your message in about fifteen minutes."

Alvin's mouth fell open. He leaned over the bed.

"My guess," said Mr. Link slowly, as though he were thinking aloud, "is that this is a simple substitution cipher. Don't let those words throw you. It merely means, if I'm right, that you've invented a new symbol for each letter of the alphabet, just like inventing a new alphabet. You've invented a new symbol for A, and used it whenever there's an A in the message.

"Also, I'll bet you've kept the word and sentence groups intact. It seems likely that those lines going up and down are used to separate the words. And whenever you come to the end of a sentence, you insert two of them. Those are my first two guesses, and breaking codes is a matter of making good guesses, then testing to see if you are right."

Mr. Link made a list of several of the symbols on the pad of paper. "These symbols here"—he pointed to the **✗◨◖◗** —"appear more frequently than the others. The four letters that appear most frequently in the English language are E, T, A, and O. They are the first four letters of what is called the Frequency Table of the English Language. The complete order is ETAON-RISHDLFCMUGYPWBVKXJQZ. In a message this short, you can't be sure that letters will appear with average frequency, but I'll at least make a guess that **✗** is the letter E." On a separate sheet of paper he marked the letter E and opposite it placed the symbol **✗** .

"There are several one-letter words in this message. What are the one-letter words in the English language?"

"A," said the Pest, "like *a* fish."

"I," said Shoie.

"Right. Those are the only ones. Now, the single-letter words in the secret message are ⌐ and ⟩. So we put these down on our 'thinking' sheet." He wrote:

⌐ = A or I
⟩ = A or I

"Now take a look at the last word in the message. It's at the bottom, below all the others. Any guesses as to what that could mean?"

"A signature?" asked Shoie.

"That's a good guess, Q-3. There are five symbols in that final word and five letters in Alvin's name. My guess is that he signed this message himself. And half the battle of breaking a code is knowing what the message *may* contain and something about the sender. So we'll fill in those symbols, with the corresponding letters in Alvin's name, on our 'thinking' sheet."

Alvin began wiggling uncomfortably beside the bed.

"Now, if we have guessed right about the signature, we know that this symbol"—he pointed to ⟩ —"is I, because it appears in Alvin's name. Therefore, we don't have to guess anymore about I and A. We *know* both of them."

He made the correction on his "thinking" paper.

"There are a couple of words that offer other clues. Take a look at these two words in the secret message." He pointed the tip of the pencil at ✗◘◘╌ and ⊏◘◘◡○.

"The same symbol appears twice in both these words. Furthermore, that same symbol is one of the most frequently used in the entire message. From our Frequency Table we can guess that the symbol is either O or T. Any guesses as to which it might be?"

"I'll bet it's O," said Shoie excitedly. "You don't often see T twos, I mean two T's in the middle of a short word."

"Right you are. At least, I think you're right. Now, take one more look at the message, and I think we're about ready to read it."

Alvin gulped.

"This symbol"—Mr. Link pointed to ○ —"appears quite frequently on the ends of words. Can you guess what it might be?"

The Pest shouted, "S. S, because that's how, when you want to make more than one of lots of words, you put on the end of. Well, you know what I mean."

"Right. Now, let's see how much progress we've made. We know—or at least have made some mighty sharp guesses —that we can identify the following letters: E, A, I, L, V, N, O, and S. Let's go just a bit farther. This word"—he pointed to ○✗✗ "appears twice. We know it ends in E. What could this word be?"

"The," said Shoie.

"She," said the Pest.

"Right. Either one is a good possibility. But whichever it is, the *second* letter probably is H. So we have another letter to add to our list. The fifth word of the message is a four-letter word, and we know the last three letters now. They are HIS. This word," he smiled, "could only be the word THIS. So we can add T to our list. Now, we think we know all of the following letters: E, A, I, L, V, N, O, S, H, and T. Let's fill them in on the secret message."

Rapidly, he wrote the letters over the symbols in the message. As he did, the message seemed to fall apart. Entire words appeared, and, in other cases, the words were so close to being solved that it was obvious what they were. Each time Mr. Link discovered a new letter in this way, he added it to his "thinking" sheet. Within three minutes he had filled in the entire message.

"Alvin," he said, "here's your secret message that's no longer so secret. It says:

IF YOU CAN DECODE THIS YOU MUST BE THE BEST DECODER IN THE WORLD. I WOULD LIKE TO LEARN JUST AS MUCH ABOUT SECRET CODES AS I POSSIBLY CAN. SHOIE AND I ARE SECRET AGENTS AND WE NEED A GOOD CODE TO SEND

MESSAGES. DO YOU KNOW OF ANY GOOD
BOOKS WE CAN READ.

ALVIN

"The answer to your question, Alvin, is yes. There
are not many good books on codes and the breaking of
codes, but there are two of them at the Riverton public
library. I presented these books to the library years ago,
from my collection."

The Magnificent Brain was bruised and befogged
by the apparent ease with which Mr. Link had broken
the cipher. "I'll get them tomorrow," said Alvin lamely.
"I'm going to study them from cover to cover, then set
up my own secret code room. It will have Frequency
Tables and everything else in it. Maybe this cipher
wasn't so hot, but I'll make one that is."

"I admire your determination. That's one of the
necessary qualities of a good cryptographer. Now suppose we set up a secret cipher between the four of us
that can't be broken by anyone without some training.
We can use it if we ever want to pass secret messages."

Mr. Link picked up his pencil and wrote the following message on the pad of paper:

APENN YSAVE DISAP ENNYE ARNED

"Can you read what that says?"

"It's a secret code, all right," said Alvin. "Maybe I
could break it if I went after it with a Frequency

Table."

Mr. Link laughed. "Actually, it's in straight English. There's no cipher at all. Look at it again. It says, A PENNY SAVED IS A PENNY EARNED. All I've done is break the words apart into different groups. We are so accustomed to seeing words as units that we don't recognize them when they are not in those units."

"I see the message," said the Pest. "Now can I be a Secret Agent, Alvin, with a number for a name?"

Alvin didn't even answer her.

"We'll divide our private cipher messages into five-letter words," continued Mr. Link. "Most messages don't come out to *exactly* five-letter groups, so we'll add X's at the end, to fill out the last group. Incidentally, such extra letters are called 'nulls' by cryptographers. Then, to confuse counterspies even more, we'll substitute numbers for the letters. We could start with 1 meaning the letter A, but let's completely confuse our enemies."

Rapidly, he wrote out a chart on a piece of paper:

A = 3	H =10	O = 17	V = 24
B = 4	I = 11	P = 18	W =25
C = 5	J = 12	Q = 19	X = 26
D = 6	K= 13	R = 20	Y = 1
E = 7	L = 14	S = 21	Z = 2
F = 8	M =15	T = 22	
G = 9	N = 16	U = 23	

"Now we have a cipher that's easy to remember and fairly difficult—without training—to solve. Let's put our secret message, 'A penny saved is a penny earned,' into this cipher. We'll be confusing the enemy by breaking the words up into difficult-to-recognize groups and by using numbers instead of letters. Here's the result:"—he held up the pad of paper—

3-18-7-16-16   1-21-3-24-7   6-11-21-3-18
7-16-16-1-7   3-20-16-7-6

"And it still says, 'A penny saved is a penny earned,' " he added.

"Wow!" said Alvin. "Nobody would be able to break *that* cipher!"

"A good cryptographer could practically read it as is," said Mr. Link with a smile. "But there are very few trained cryptographers in the world, so I think our messages will be fairly safe in this cipher. We can reconstruct this cipher anytime we want, without any code book. Now what do we have to remember?"

"First, we break the message into five-letter words, no matter how many letters there really are in the words," said Shoie.

"Then we write down the alphabet with a number next to each letter, starting with A meaning 3," said Alvin.

"Then we give the message to me to deliver," said the Pest. "And if I get caught, I chew it up and swallow it!"

"How about some popcorn instead?" asked Mrs. Murphy, appearing in the doorway.

CHAPTER 8

Adventure in the Library

AFTER school, a few days later, a rather strange sign appeared over the door to Alvin's bedroom. It was carefully lettered in red poster paint. Alvin was in such a hurry that he tacked up the sign before some of the letters were dry, and as a result the paint had droozled down across the door frame, as though the last word were bleeding to death. In addition, Alvin was not a good speller.

The sign said:

ALVIN FERNALD, CRIPTOGRUFFER

Alvin looked up at the sign with satisfaction, then assembled the tools of his new trade. He swept the clutter off his desk, sharpened a dozen pencils until their points were like needles, and got out a pad of ruled paper to use as his worksheet. Now, he was ready.

From experience, he knew that the Magnificent

Brain clicked away at its highest speed when his feet were higher than his head. He spent ten minutes sliding the bed back and forth, carefully adjusting it so that when he sat in his chair and tilted way back with his feet on the desk the back of the chair was supported by the bed. It was a good position, and he wondered why he'd never thought of it before.

Alvin Fernald, Criptogruffer, was ready for business.

It was then that it occurred to Alvin that he wasn't being completely honest with himself. If he were going to be a cryptographer, he needed two things:

A. Customers.

B. A great deal more knowledge of codes and ciphers than he had learned in his two visits to Mr. Link.

Later, he'd figure out how to get customers. Now, he had to learn more about codes. Just about then, his mother called him to dinner.

At the table he said, "Mom, can I go down to the library tonight?"

"*May* I," corrected the Pest.

Alvin gave her a nasty look.

"Yes, you *may* go," said his mother, emphasizing the word, "if someone else goes along. I don't want you roaming around alone after dark."

"I'll go," said the Pest.

Alvin gave her another nasty look. "Shoie will go along."

"While you're at the library," said his dad with a twinkle in his eye, "you'd better check out a spelling book or two. That sign over your bedroom door proves that you aren't the world's greatest speller."

The Pest said brightly, "The word should be spelled c-r-y-p-t-o-g-r-a-p-h-e-r. Cryptographer."

"Good heavens, Daphne," said their mom. "How did you ever learn to spell a word that long?"

"Alvin and I are going into the cryptography business. We're going to solve mysterious codes."

Alvin gave her a really nasty look.

"If you kids are going to solve mysteries," said their dad, "I wish you'd solve Miss Fenwick's mystery."

Through a mouthful of mashed potatoes, Alvin asked, "Have you found Mr. Smith, who wrote her that letter?"

"Nope. Not a sign of any stranger in town named Smith. I checked the hotels and motels. Miss Fenwick is pretty discouraged. She's planning to leave this weekend."

"She's a lovely woman," said Mrs. Fernald. "For her own sake, as well as those orphans, I hope she finds some money *someplace*, even though it isn't a buried treasure."

"Maybe," said Alvin, "she ought to take a hundred bulldozers out there to Treasure Bluffs and level the whole place. She might find the treasure that way."

Sergeant Fernald laughed. "I'm afraid there wouldn't be much hope of success. No one knows for sure that a buried treasure even exists."

"Tell her to wait until this weekend," said Alvin. "I'll go out there and look over the bluffs myself. Maybe I can find the treasure for her."

"If anybody can, I'll bet on you, Alvin," said his Dad.

The Riverton public library was really an old home, presented to the town many years ago. It was a two-story structure, complete with odd little turrets and towers, set in the middle of the landscaped grounds maintained by the Ladies Rose Society. A high iron fence ran all the way around the grounds. There was only one gate, at the front.

Miss Jackson stood behind the desk, busily stamping books with her nimble fingers, when Alvin, Shoie, and the Pest walked in. For twenty-five years, she had been the librarian.

As she glanced up, a disturbed look crossed her face, but she smiled and waved at them. Alvin knew the reason for the disturbed look. Whenever he came to the library something seemed to happen, although he was darned if he could figure out why these disasters were his fault.

Once, while standing on a stool among the long rows of shelves, he'd lost his balance. When he fell, he'd knocked over the big bookshelf in front of him; it had crashed into the next one and, in a chain reaction, down went half the shelves in the library, like a big row of dominoes. When Alvin had scrambled up out of the depths of the books, it looked like an earthquake had struck the building.

He'd looked over at Miss Jackson. She was standing there behind the desk, stunned, her whole world toppled to the floor at her feet. She turned her head slowly until she saw him. Then she put her finger to her lips and pointed a pencil at the sign behind the desk. It said SILENCE. Immediately afterward she'd started to laugh. She'd laughed so loud and so long that Alvin thought there might be something wrong with her. But, with tears running down her face, she came over and put her arm around him. Still laughing, she gasped, "Alvin Fernald, that's the first exciting thing that's happened in this library in twenty years. It will take a week to straighten out this mess, but it's worth it."

Another time, he'd walked through the front door to return some books. Miss Jackson had looked up and said, "Alvin, take that cat out of here." Until then, Alvin hadn't known there was a cat in there. Sure enough, at his feet was a big gray cat that had followed him through the door. As he reached down for it, the cat had streaked away through the shelves. Alvin ran after it, past a startled Mr. Ufer, who had been quietly reading, his bald head glistening under one of the table lamps. It had taken Alvin three minutes to corner the cat, and then he found it crouched on a top shelf, snarling down at him. As he lunged upward for it, it leaped wildly through the air and landed smack on top of Mr. Ufer's head, sliding off the smooth surface and landing with a thump right between the pages of the book Mr. Ufer had been reading.

Therefore, it was not surprising that a disturbed look crossed Miss Jackson's face when she saw Alvin enter the library, followed by Shoie and the Pest. They marched straight up to the desk.

"Hi, Miss Jackson," said Alvin.

"Shh," she said, gesturing toward a man seated at a nearby table. He was a big man, whose head seemed to settle down into his body without any neck. Alvin noticed that he needed a shave. Books and papers were scattered across the table in front of him.

"Hi, Miss Jackson," repeated Alvin, this time in a very low whisper.

"Hello, Alvin. Hi, kids," she whispered back. "Be careful of the shelves and the cats." She always said that; it was a standing joke between them.

"We're studying up on codes and how to break them," whispered Alvin. "Do you have any good books?"

"We have a couple of fine ones. They were donated to the library by Mr. Link. Just a second." She pulled out the small drawer of a card file, riffled through the cards, and wrote some numbers on a slip of paper. "Here are their catalog numbers. You'll find them over in those stacks." She waved her hand toward the far corner.

Years ago, Miss Jackson had taught Alvin how to use the catalog numbers to find any book in the library. Now it suddenly occurred to Alvin that the numbers were, in a way, a code. Anyone who had learned the code could quickly find a particular book among the thousands in the library.

On the way back to the stacks, the kids passed the big man hunched over the table. He didn't even look up at them.

Alvin led the way through the long shelves until at last he came to a particular section. He looked carefully along the shelves until he came to the spot where the two code books should be stored. He couldn't find them. Checking the numbers on the slip of paper, he looked once more.

"They aren't here," he announced in a whisper.

"Maybe Miss Jackson made a mistake," suggested the Pest.

"Miss Jackson never makes mistakes," countered Shoie.

Alvin looked again. This time he noticed that there was a gap in the shelves, just large enough for two books, in the exact spot where the code books should be.

"Somebody has them out," he said. Then he thought a moment. "That's strange. I'll bet Miss Jackson knows who's taken out almost any book in this library. And I'll bet those code books aren't checked out very often. Seems like she'd know if they had been checked out."

"Maybe somebody stole them," said the Pest.

"We'd better talk to her," said Alvin.

Back they marched toward the desk. As they passed the big man at the table, Alvin glanced down, then stopped so suddenly that the other two bumped into him, sending him reeling into a reading lamp that came up through the table. There was a loud pop, the tinkle of glass, and a blinding flash of light. The big man sprang to his feet and started brushing the pieces of the broken bulb off his clothing.

Alvin looked over at Miss Jackson. She shook her head sadly, as though she had been expecting it to happen.

"I'm sorry," she called over to the man, who was peering angrily at Alvin from beneath heavy eyebrows. "Don't try to clean it up. The library will be swept out as soon as we close. Why don't you move to another table?"

"I'm sorry, too," said Alvin.

The man snatched up a book and some of the loose papers, and began moving them to another table. When Alvin picked up one of his books and an old piece of paper from the table to help him, the man grabbed them out of his hand. "Why don't you watch what you're doing?" he said.

Alvin nudged Shoie and looked at the Pest. "Come

on back to the stacks."

In the far corner, among the shelves, he began whispering excitedly. "Did you see what that man was doing?"

"Studying," said Q-3.

"Right," said Alvin. "But, old bean, did you notice what he was studying?"

"Arithmetic," said the Pest. "He had a lot of numbers and letters written on those papers in front of him."

Alvin said, very slowly for emphasis, "The two books on that table are the code books we're looking for. And on those sheets of paper are a lot of scribbles that don't make sense. On the old piece of paper that he snatched out of my hand, there are a lot of letters in neat little rows. *That man is trying to break a secret code!*"

"Wow!" said Q-3. "Are you sure?"

"Gosh!" whispered the Pest.

The Magnificent Brain suddenly shifted into high gear with such a jolt that Alvin hit the side of his head with his palm. The thought was an exciting one, so exciting that he couldn't even speak. Then Alvin Fernald, schoolboy, became Fernald, Inc., Master Counterspy and Criptogruffer.

"I'll tell you something else," he said dramatically, as though proclaiming one of the secrets of the universe. "That man out there is the mysterious Mr. Smith. And that old piece of paper he has in front of him is a code message, written way back during the Civil War, that tells exactly where Miss Fenwick's treasure is buried!"

"How do you know?" asked Shoie doubtfully.

"It's the only explanation that makes sense. A Mr. Smith wrote a mysterious letter to Miss Fenwick from Riverton, so there *must* be a Mr. Smith around here somewhere—even though that may not be his real name. And remember what Miss Fenwick told us? The bushwhacker, Blacky, who killed Mr. Moses and buried the treasure, had been a Union spy. That means he'd know all about secret codes. When he buried the treasure, he had to know where to find it again. So he wrote down the location. But to protect his secret, he wrote the location in code."

"Maybe," said Shoie, still doubtful, "but then how did Mr. Smith get the code message?"

"That we don't know," said Alvin. "But we can guess one other thing. Our mysterious Mr. Smith can't read that secret message or he wouldn't be studying code books in the Riverton public library. I'll bet he's trying to learn how to break codes."

"Let's go home and tell your dad," said Shoie. "I speel kind of fooky. I mean I feel kind of spooky."

"Not yet," said K-21 1/2. "First, we have to get a copy of that secret message."

"How are you going to do that?"

"I'm not. *You* are."

"*You* are," repeated the Pest.

Shoie grabbed one of the shelves, as though he needed support. "Doggone it. You get some of the wildest ideas, Alvin. How am I going to get that message? He's bigger than I am!"

"You let me take care of that. Now listen. Here's what you do. Take a book off the shelf and go sit down at the same table with him. I'll get him away from the table. While he's gone, you copy off the secret message. Don't pay any attention to the other papers on the table. Just the one that looks very old and very dirty. Copy it off *exactly* as it looks, even though it doesn't make sense. Got it?"

"Got it. But I don't like it."

"Okay. Go to it." Alvin took a book at random from a shelf. The title was *Metaphysical Aspects of Existentialism.* "You read some pretty deep stuff," he whispered with a smile, as he handed it to Shoie.

Trying to appear nonchalant, Shoie sauntered over and sat down across from the man. He opened the book and began reading as though he could hardly wait to devour the next word.

"He's holding the book upside down," whispered the Pest.

Alvin popped out from the shelves, carrying a couple of books, and walked over to stand beside Shoie. Meanwhile, the Pest went over and started talking to Miss Jackson, to keep her from noticing what was going on.

"Good book?" Alvin asked Shoie in a voice just a bit too loud.

The man looked up. "Shut up!" he growled. That

was all he said, but his eyes seemed to see right through to the back of Alvin's skull. A shiver ran down K-21 1/2's back.

"Sorry," he said. Then, looking down casually at the top of the table, "Oh, *you* have the books I was looking for. The ones on secret codes, I mean. No hurry, but I'd like to see them when you're through."

"Get out of here, kid," snapped the man.

"Sorry," said Alvin again. "I was just looking for books on secret codes. There's only one other in the library, but it's not on *making* codes. It's on *breaking* them."

The man looked up quickly. For the first time, there was interest on his face. "You say there's a book here on how to *break* codes?"

"Yep. But I don't want that one. All I want is . . ."

"Where is it?" the man broke in.

"Back there in the shelves. Saw it just a minute ago. But I don't want . . ."

"Can you find it for me?"

"Sure," said Alvin. "Glad to." He glanced meaningfully at Shoie, then walked back toward the shelves. He heard the scrape of a chair behind him, but didn't dare look back to see whether the man had gathered his papers off the table.

As soon as he got to the shelves, Alvin raced completely around one row and ducked up another aisle. Now, he had to gain time, time so Shoie could copy the message. He heard the man walking down the rows, looking for him. Alvin stepped quietly around to the third aisle. Moments passed. Then, when he heard footsteps approaching, he tipped one of the books forward, as though he were reading the title.

"Hi," he said as the man walked up. "I think it's right around here somewhere."

The man looked at him suspiciously. "Are you trying to fool me, kid?"

"No. I saw it right along here." Alvin continued to look through the books.

"What's the name of it?" growled the man.

"Let's see." The Magnificent Brain thought furiously. "If I remember right, the title is *A Master Spy's Secrets of Breaking Codes and Ciphers*, written by Alvin Fernald."

Suddenly, the man grabbed Alvin's arm. "What's your game, kid?" he hissed. "All the shelves in this section are covered with chemistry books. You know there isn't any book on codes here. What are you up to?"

Panic began to seep through Alvin's mind. He said the first thing that came into his head, the words tumbling out one after the other. He *had* to gain time so Shoie could copy the message. "There is too such a book. It was given to the library by Mr. Link. He lives over on Fourth Street. He was a spy in World War II, and he knows all about breaking secret codes. He can break any code there is. And he told me about this book that's here in the library. I can't help it if I made a mistake about where the book is. Maybe it's on the next row of shelves. Let go my arm, mister, you're hurting . . ."

Just then, the man *did* let go. He whirled around and blundered out through the stacks. In that split second Alvin knew what had happened. The man had suddenly realized he'd left his secret message unguarded.

Alvin raced down another aisle at top speed. He rounded the corner just as the man came out from behind the shelves.

"Run, Shoie!" shouted Alvin, heading toward the door himself.

He saw Shoie leap to his feet, crumple a piece of paper in front of him, and slip it into his pocket. Out of the corner of his eye he saw Miss Jackson, still talking to the Pest, glance up with wide eyes. The Pest started running, too.

Shoie, the mighty athlete, reached the door first. Right at his heels was the Pest, and Alvin brought up the rear. As Alvin darted through the door, he glanced back over his shoulder. The man had paused at the table just long enough to snatch up the old scrap of paper. Then he too was running toward the door.

Outside, the street light splashed a tiny pool of light down on the empty sidewalk. Shoie and the Pest were halfway to the front gate when Alvin heard the big man pounding along behind him. In mid-stride, he thought of a plan of escape. Searching desperately through his pockets, he pulled out the wrapper from an old jelly sandwich. He glanced over his shoulder. By now, the man was only fifteen feet away.

Waving the wrapper wildly, Alvin yelled, "I've got a copy of that message!" Then he veered suddenly, and instead of heading for the gate, he ran for his life around the library.

With every step that he took, he could hear the man gaining. When they reached the back of the library, it was apparent in the bright moonlight that there was no opening in the high iron fence, except the front gate on the other side of the building.

"Got you now!" muttered the man.

Alvin imagined fingers on the back of his neck, but he knew something that the man didn't know. For years, he had been crawling between the bars at the corner of the fence to get to the library. Lately, since he had grown so much, it had become a sort of a test to him. Could he still squeeze through or not? The last time he'd tried was about six months ago.

He dived through some bushes that grew just inside the fence and heard the branches snap back and hit the man in the face, slowing him temporarily. Now Alvin was at the corner of the fence. For the first time, he knew exactly how a trapped animal must feel. Poking his head through the iron bars, he wriggled one shoulder through. Suddenly, he was stuck. He looked up in the dim light to see the man charging out of the bushes.

With a last desperate heave, Alvin wrenched himself through the bars. For just a moment, he felt fingers on the bottom of his jacket. He tugged and freed himself, then ran a few steps. Suddenly, he stopped and turned around. He knew he was safe now.

The man stood with his hands squeezing the bars of the fence. It was obvious he couldn't get through, and just as obvious that there was no way to climb the high fence. He stood there, pure hatred in his eyes as he looked at Alvin.

"I'm going to find you," the man said slowly and softly. "I'm going to find you and take care of you good. I don't know why you're meddling in my business, but you've meddled just a little too much. You'd better keep looking back over your shoulder, because sometime soon I'll be there."

Alvin felt a chill crawl up his spine. He turned and ran for home. On the way, he ducked down every alley he could find.

And, sure enough, he kept looking back over his shoulder.

CHAPTER 9

Alvin Fernald, Criptogruffer

S HOIE and the Pest were waiting on the front steps.

"Oh, Alvin!" said the Pest. "We were so worried!"

"Hurry! Come on inside," said Alvin, looking over his shoulder down the dark street.

They headed straight up the stairs for Alvin's room.

"Did you find what you wanted at the library?" called his mother from the living room.

Alvin put a finger to his lips, warning the others. "Yes, Mom."

"Shoie better go home soon. Bedtime before long."

"Okay, Mom. We're just going up and talk for a minute. Then he'll head for home."

They walked under the sign, ALVIN FERNALD, CRIPTOGRUFFER, and Alvin closed the door behind them.

"Alvin, we were so worried about you," said the Pest again.

"How'd you get away, old bean?" asked Shoie.

He told them, and he felt himself shuddering as he described the man on the other side of the fence. "That man is dangerous," he said.

The Pest was worried. "Alvin, hadn't we better tell Daddy?"

"I've been thinking about that. I don't think we should—yet. After all, we *were* meddling with *his* papers. There's no way anybody can *prove* he is the mysterious Mr. Smith. Dad couldn't arrest him, just for sitting in the library."

"What are we going to do, old bean?" asked Shoie. "I don't want to walk the streets with that guy looking for me."

"I was wrong a minute ago when I said there's no way to prove that he's involved with the treasure. There *is* a way, one way."

"What's that?"

"Suppose," said Alvin slowly, "suppose we could break the code message that we got from him. And suppose it tells us where to find the treasure. And suppose we find the treasure, by using the message, before he does. That will be mighty strong evidence that he's the mysterious Mr. Smith who wrote Miss Fenwick." The more Alvin talked, the more excited he became. "Shoie, let's take a look at your copy of the message!"

From his pocket Shoie produced the crumpled

piece of paper. They smoothed it on the bed. In Shoie's desperate scrawl appeared a jumble of letters:

```
SREWO  TETIN  ARGNE EWTEB  GIDDN  ASECA
PEVLE  WTTHG  IRNRU TKCOR  DAEHE  LTRUT
OTHTR  ONOGT  SEWHT RONTS  EWSEC  APNEE
TFIFO  GREDL  UOBEG RALMO  RFFFU  LBTSE
PEETS  FOESA  BTALO OPRET  AWRAE  LCDNI
FSFFU  LBREV  IROTS ELIME  ERHTT  SEWHT
UOSEK  IRTSA  NAIDN INOTR  EVIRD  ELLAC
EGALL  IVOTO  GXXXX
```

"Gosh," said the Pest, "who could read that?"

Alvin looked at Shoie. "You'd better head for home, old bean. There's not much we can do tonight. And be careful on the way."

Then, Alvin Fernald, Criptogruffer, turned and answered the Pest's question. "I can read the secret message," he said simply.

Alvin spent a restless night. In a nightmare, he was running down a dark street, looking back over his shoulder at huge letters that were chasing him.

Even though it was a bad night, he could hardly wait to attack the code. He tried to do it once in school the next day, behind his social studies book, but when Miss Peppersmith began looking rather strangely at him, he hid the coded message between the pages.

At last, Miss Peppersmith closed the books on her

desk and placed them neatly between the bookends. It was Friday afternoon and, as the bell rang, the warm squishy feeling suddenly flowed into Alvin's stomach once more, this time heightened by the feeling that something was about to happen.

Shoie had to rake leaves, so Alvin went alone to his secret code room. He sat down and attacked the code.

Each part of the message had five letters in it, so it was obvious the message was not split into regular words. This would make a solution more difficult. On the other hand, certain letters appeared more frequently than others. He decided to run a letter-frequency check on some of the letters, just as Mr. Link had done. It took half an hour, but when he was through, he felt he had made some progress:

E-32	L-13
T-25	I-12
R-19	N-11
O-17	F-9
A-14	D-7
S-13	H-6

Alvin grinned with satisfaction. Lining up the

letters in order, he wrote just beneath them the first dozen letters of the Frequency Table:

ETROASLINFDH
ETAONRISHDLF

He knew from Mr. Link that unless the message was extremely long, it would not match the Frequency Table *exactly*. But this came mighty close.

He was certain, now, that the letters stood for themselves and not some other letters of the alphabet. They apparently were scrambled in some way. He worked for an hour, but still could make no sense out of the message.

Desperately, he reviewed again what Mr. Link had told him, seeking a clue that would lead to the solution. Messages, Mr. Link had said once, are much easier to decipher if you know something about the man who has coded them and about the situation in which the message was written. Thoughtfully, Alvin made a list of everything he knew about the man and the situation:

1. Blacky was a former spy and would know a lot about codes.
2. Blacky was burying a treasure, so it seemed likely that the message was full of directions; something like "go southeast" or "measure fifteen feet."
3. Blacky was in a desperate hurry when he wrote the

message. He had to do it fast because, in order to keep his secret, he had to catch up with Mr. Moses and prevent him from talking.

It seemed to Alvin that the last point was particularly important. If Blacky was in such a hurry, he couldn't take time to make a complicated code or cipher. It had to be simple; some cipher he could use in a hurry so he could get on the trail of Mr. Moses. If this were true, the cipher should be fairly easy to solve.

Despite this reasoning, the letters still appeared to be scrambled beyond understanding. There wasn't a five-letter group that seemed to make any sense. He finally gave up, temporarily, and went outside to clear the cobwebs from the Magnificent Brain. But as soon as he was outside, halfheartedly tossing the basketball at the backboard on the garage, he found himself peering back over his shoulder. He returned to the house, somewhat ashamed of himself.

The Pest was in the kitchen with Mrs. Fernald, rolling out pie crusts. Alvin noticed that the Pest, too, was sticking close to home.

Late in the afternoon the problem had become so irritating that he returned to his room, locked the door, and once again attacked the code. He *had* to solve it, for a good many reasons. The most important was that he had boasted that he could. Still, the letters seemed to dance in front of his eyes.

What else had Mr. Link said? He couldn't remember the exact quotation, but it was something like "nothing can be so baffling as simplicity." There *had* to be a simple answer to this code. Maybe he'd been trying to make it too complicated. If he were in Blacky's shoes, how would he encode the message in a hurry and in a very simple yet puzzling way?

He snatched up the message once more, and this time words began to swim in front of his eyes. They didn't make sense at first, but now it was almost within his grasp.

Then, suddenly, he had the key! He knew how to find the buried treasure!

Just as suddenly, he was afraid the cipher was *too* simple. It seemed impossible that Mr. Smith couldn't solve it, just by looking at it. Still, if he hadn't solved it yet, it probably would baffle him for a little longer.

His dad was calling him to dinner. On the way to the table, Alvin called Shoie. "This is K-21 1/2. Come over as soon as you've finished dinner. It's important."

He was so excited that he barely touched his dinner. His mother fussed over him, and even went so far as to take his temperature.

Shoie showed up as it was growing dark. The two boys immediately went to Alvin's room. The Pest squeezed through the door behind them.

Alvin stood beside his decoding desk. In a voice trembling with triumph, he said, "Alvin Fernald, cryptographer, has broken the cipher. I know where the treasure is buried!"

CHAPTER 10

The Captives

"ALVIN! Have you really broken the cipher?" asked the Pest.

"Do you really know where the treasure is buried?" asked Shoie.

Alvin drew himself to his full height, which was still half a head shorter than Shoie. "Yes. I, Agent K-21 1/2, have solved the cipher and can find the treasure."

"Quick! Where is it, old bean? Let's go find it."

"Let's tell Dad right away, Alvin. Then let's get Miss Fenwick and go dig it up for all her orphans."

Alvin was quiet for a moment. When he spoke, his voice had the ring of authority in it. "No. No, we're not going to find the treasure just yet."

"Why not?" asked Shoie.

"Because there's something we should do first. We owe somebody for all the time he's spent with us. He's *really* the one who broke the code and solved the secret message. He taught me how to do it."

"Mr. Link," said Shoie.

"Exactly. Mr.Link. And I want him to be the first to know all about the secret message."

"But maybe somebody will get there first!" exclaimed the Pest. "Maybe somebody else will discover the treasure."

"Nope. That treasure has been buried in the same spot for more than a hundred years. I don't think anyone will stumble across it in the next hour. There's only one man, the mysterious Mr. Smith, who knows anything about it, and he doesn't know anything about breaking codes, or he would have broken this one long ago." Alvin grabbed his old baseball cap out of the closet. "Come on. Let's go tell Mr. Link right now."

Sergeant Fernald never permitted them to ride their bikes after dark, so they walked over to Mr. Link's house. All the way over, the Pest danced excitedly around the two boys, wondering how much the treasure would be worth and exactly what they'd find.

Halfway up Mr. Link's walk, Alvin paused for a moment. "That's funny," he said in a low voice.

"What's funny?" asked Shoie.

"The only light in the house is in Mr. Link's room. You'd think that Mrs. Murphy would have a light on somewhere else in the house."

"Maybe she's gone downtown," suggested Shoie.

"The stores are closed tonight."

"Maybe so," said Alvin, but there was a doubtful note in his voice. "You kids wait here for just a minute. I'm going around to the side of the house. Something seems wrong to me, and maybe I can find out what it is."

"It isn't nice to look in people's windows," the Pest reminded him.

"I'll just take one look, to make sure everything's okay. Be right back."

Alvin walked across the grass, black in the night. The air was already chilly with a hint of the coming winter. He hunched his shoulders inside his jacket and jammed his hands into his pockets to keep them warm.

As he rounded the corner of the house, he still had the uneasy feeling that something was wrong. Even in Mr. Link's room, only one light was on, the one over the bed, he thought. He pushed aside the bushes around the foundation of the house, and stood on tiptoe to see into the room.

The window had been left open about six inches. Through this gap Alvin saw a sight that made his heart leap into his throat. Mr. Link was leaning back against his pillow. And standing right beside him was the mysterious Mr. Smith!

For a moment, Alvin's mind was a jumble of confused thoughts. He shook his head, trying to clear it. Finally, one clear thought came through, an ugly thought. *Mr. Link was helping Mr. Smith break the code to find the treasure!*

He could scarcely believe it. Still, the more he watched, the more convinced he became that Mr. Link was working on the code. He was writing rapidly on a pad of paper in his lap, and all over the bed were discarded sheets. As Alvin watched, Mr. Smith reached his big hand across and picked up a scrap of paper from the bed. In the clear cone of light from the bed lamp, Alvin could see that it was the yellowed piece of paper with the treasure message written on it.

So they *were* working together.

Mr. Smith looked up at the window, and Alvin once more had the feeling that the man was staring straight into the back of his skull. Apparently, he couldn't see into the darkness beyond the window, though, for he leaned over to see more clearly what Mr. Link was writing on the sheet of paper.

Suddenly, something bumped Alvin's arm. He was so startled he had to choke down a shout, and, glancing around, he found Shoie and the Pest standing beside him in the bushes.

"What's the matter, Alvin?" asked the Pest in a loud voice. "You were gone so long we were afraid that . . ."

"Shhh!" he hissed, clamping his hand roughly over her mouth.

She started to struggle, then thought better of it and stood absolutely motionless beneath the window.

"What's going on, old bean?" whispered Shoie.

Kneeling beside the house, he told them in a low voice everything he'd seen. "So you see," he ended, "Mr. Link must be helping break the code and read the secret message."

"And I thought Mr. Link was such a nice man," whispered the Pest. "We'd better tell Daddy right away."

"We will," agreed Alvin. "But first I want to find out whether they're making any progress in breaking the code."

"How're we going to do that?" asked Shoie. "Dock on the noor and ask them?"

"If I can only hear what they're saying, we'll know how they're making out." He looked up at the window. "Q-3, I'm going to get up to that window and listen. And you're going to be my ladder." He gave Shoie a gentle shove over toward the foundation, just beneath the window.

"What if they catch us," whispered the Pest.

"Then run like you've never run before."

Alongside the foundation, the two boys looked up into the black night, pierced by the glow from the window.

"Stoop over and put your hands on your knees," said Alvin.

Q-3 leaned over. When Alvin put a knee in the middle of his back, he staggered against the foundation.

"Hold still!"

"I never realized you were so heavy. What did you eat for dinner? Lead?"

Alvin carefully planted both knees in the middle of Shoie's back, then lifted himself to his feet, leaning against the side of the house for support. Beneath him, Shoie grunted and swayed, trying to keep his balance.

Straightening to his full height, Alvin found himself outlined against the window. Quickly, he squatted back down, afraid he had been seen, then slowly raised his head.

Inside the room, Mr. Link was still working on the code. Mr. Smith was standing beside him, his face screwed into an ugly, impatient look. Through the gap beneath the window, Alvin could hear their voices.

"Come on," Mr. Smith was saying, "you can do better than that. That kid at the library told me you were an expert."

There was a long pause. Then Mr. Link replied, "This is a very difficult code to break. I'll need time."

"Well, keep working. I want to be able to read that message tonight."

Beneath Alvin's feet, Shoie stirred restlessly. Alvin looked down into the blackness, but after staring into the lighted room, he couldn't see a thing. "Hold still," he whispered softly, cupping one hand to his mouth so the sound wouldn't carry into the room.

"Glug," said Shoie. "Gunchasnee!"

"What?"

"Gunchasnee," whispered Shoie. Then he sniffled.

"Gunchasnee!" His voice sounded strangled.

"I can't understand what you're saying, old man."

"Gunchasnee!" said Shoie desperately. "Glug! Gunna snee! Going to sneeze!"

The last words were perfectly clear, and speared Alvin to the heart. He raised himself quickly to take one last look. Then, beneath him, Alvin felt Shoie's back shudder convulsively.

"SCHEEEEEWWWWW!" Shoie tried to strangle the sneeze in his throat. The effort was so great that he staggered violently away from the foundation.

Alvin had one last view of the room as he started to fall. Mr. Smith's back was turned, but Mr. Link was looking straight at the window, straight into Alvin's eyes. Then he was falling, crashing through the bushes. He put out both hands, hit with a thud, and found his thumb squashing Shoie's nose over to one side.

"Too late," said Shoie.

"Too late for what?"

"No sense putting your hand over my nose now. I've already sneezed."

Their legs were so tangled that neither of them could rise. "We'd better get out of here quick," said Alvin. "Mr. Link saw me through the window."

"Get off my leg!"

"*You* get off *my* leg!"

Just then the light on the porch came on, casting a pool of light out across the side yard. The Pest, who had been standing on the lawn, dived into the shelter of the bushes with the two boys.

"Too late!" whispered Alvin. "Can't get away now. Lie perfectly still!"

He felt the soft, cool dirt beneath his hands. The front door squeaked open and heavy steps came across the porch toward the side of the house. The footsteps stopped, and there was a long pause. Alvin imagined Mr. Smith's ugly face peering around the corner of the house, searching the bushes with his eyes. He squeezed the handful of dirt into a little ball.

For what seemed hours they stayed there, muscles frozen. At one point Shoie stirred and Alvin had the horrifying thought that he might be about to sneeze again. Finally, they heard the heavy footsteps retreat across the porch, and waited fearfully for the sound of feet coming down the front steps to search the yard. Instead, the front door slammed and the glow of the porch light suddenly vanished.

Quickly, Alvin and Shoie untangled themselves and stood up. For a moment they stood there, gathering their wits. Then Alvin whispered, "Let's get out of here!"

He was just scrambling out from under the bushes when he heard something drop from above. It whooshed past his ear and landed softly on the grass in front of him. *They've found us*, was his first startled thought. His hand reached out and closed around the object. It was a ball of crumpled paper. Alvin leaped to his feet.

Shoie and the Pest were already halfway across the yard. By the time they reached the sidewalk, Alvin had caught up and passed the Pest, grabbing her by the arm to hurry her along.

The three figures raced through the darkness, rounded the corner, and sped down Maple Street. Alvin called to Shoie, "Wait!" Then he stopped under a street light. Staring back down the dark street, Alvin saw no sign of Mr. Smith.

Carefully, he straightened out the ball of paper in his hand and studied it in the dim glow of the street light.

Shoie came walking back toward them. "What's the matter, Alvin? We'd better get out of here." Then he saw the piece of paper. "What do you have there?"

Alvin gazed at the paper for a long minute. Then he said, "It's a message. A message to us from Mr. Link. And it's in cipher."

"How do you know it's a message to us?" asked Shoie.

"It's in our *private* cipher, old bean. The code Mr. Link invented just for us." A note of excitement had crept into Alvin's voice. Sitting down on the curb, he dug through his jacket pockets until he found the stub of a pencil. "Keep watching down the street," he instructed. "If you see anything of Mr. Smith, holler bloody murder and start running."

Smoothing the paper over his knee, Alvin peered down at it. The point of the pencil went into his mouth, and the Magnificent Brain buzzed into action. Scrawled across the paper was a jumble of numbers:

9-7-22-10-7   14-18-19-23-11   5-13-21-22-20
3-16-9-7-20   10-17-14-6-11   16-9-23-21-18
20-11-21-17-16   7-20-15-20-21   15-23-20-18-10
1-14-17-5-13   7-6-11-16-4   3-21-7-15-7
16-22-15-3-16   25-11-14-14-10   3-20-15-10-7
20-23-16-14-7   21-21-11-6-7   5-17-6-7-15
7-21-21-3-9   7-21-22-3-14   14-11-16-9-<u>9</u>
<u>7-22-10-7-14</u> <u>18-26-26-26-26</u>

Rapidly, in accordance with the cipher they had set up, Alvin scrawled the alphabet on the paper, then numbered the letters: A = 3, B = 4, and so on. Then, he deciphered the numbers in the message into letters, and separated the groups of letters into words.

"Listen to this," he announced, his voice shaking. "Here's what the message says:

> Get help quick. Stranger holding us prisoner. Mrs. Murphy locked in basement. Man will harm her unless I decode message. Stalling. Get help.

"The last two words are underlined. Come on," shouted Alvin, leaping to his feet. "Ogilvie's drug store. Telephone!"

As usual, Shoie arrived first. By the time Alvin reached the drug store, two blocks away, the star athlete was standing inside the door, waiting, a wild look on his face. Mr. Ogilvie had looked up to see Shoie burst through the door, then a moment later Alvin hurtled through, and both boys were gasping for breath.

Alvin spotted the three phone booths at the back of the store. Quickly, he searched through his pockets, then remembered that he'd left his billfold on his desk.

"Mr. Ogilvie," he pleaded, "will you lend me four dimes until tomorrow morning? I promise I'll pay you back from my allowance." He was so excited that it didn't even occur to him to ask Mr. Ogilvie to phone for help.

The man looked at him for a long moment, then punched the "no sale" button on the cash register. With agonizing slowness he reached in, carefully counted out four dimes, counted them again, then reached across the counter and handed them to Alvin.

Back at the phone booths, Alvin gave two of the dimes to Shoie. He was so excited that one of the dimes slipped out of his hand, rolled across the floor, and disappeared under the magazine rack. Both boys scrambled after it, but only the Pest's small hand could reach under the magazine rack and retrieve the coin.

"Mr. Link needs help," gasped Alvin, still trying to catch his breath. "We'll get him lots of help. Shoie, call the police department and tell them to go to the corner of Fourth and Maple. Dad's on duty tonight, but I don't think he'll answer the phone. Don't even take time to ask for him. Just give them the message. Then call the fire department and tell them the same thing."

Alvin slipped into one of the booths, dropped a dime in the slot, and dialed the operator. When he heard her cheerful voice, he said, "Quick! Get the gas company. Tell them to go to the corner of Fourth and Maple streets immediately. Emergency!"

He slammed down the receiver, dropped in another dime, and dialed the operator again. "Quick!" he shouted. "Emergency! Tell the electric company to go to the corner of Fourth and Maple immediately. Matter of life and death!"

As Alvin came plunging out of the phone booth, Shoie slammed down the receiver and stepped out beside him. "Got them both," reported Q-3. "Police and fire departments."

"Come on," said Alvin, grabbing the Pest by the arm. "Let's go see what happens."

The three kids raced out the door.

Mr. Ogilvie, who hadn't been able to hear their words, stood behind the cash register shaking his head. Suddenly, the door reopened and Alvin's head popped in. "Thanks, Mr. Ogilvie. See you tomorrow. Forty cents I owe you." The face vanished and the door slammed shut again.

Mr. Ogilvie rubbed his eyes.

CHAPTER 11

Alvin to the Rescue

SIREN screaming, the ladder truck from the fire department arrived on the scene first. It ground to a halt smack in the middle of the intersection, and three firemen piled off. They began pulling ladders off the truck while the driver and the man beside him looked around for the fire.

The siren was just fading away when the fire engine arrived with a scream, slammed to a stop behind the ladder truck, and the men began unrolling hose across the intersection to connect it to the fire hydrant.

From the opposite direction came the howl of the police siren. It squealed to a stop in front of the ladder truck and two policemen, one of them Sergeant Fernald, leaped out. There was a great deal of confusion, with men running in all directions through the darkness, and shouts of "Where is it?" and "Who turned in the alarm?"

In the middle of the confusion, the emergency

trucks of the gas and electric companies ground to a halt, red lights blinking atop their cabs. Spotlights from all the vehicles pierced the darkness, roaming over the houses in the area.

Porch lights began winking on in the nearby homes. Fire hose was strewn about the intersection like great piles of giant spaghetti. And now came the sightseers, cars rolling to a stop from every direction as curious folk tried to find out what was going on.

From their hiding place in the bushes beside Mr. Link's house, the kids looked on in amazement. Alvin stood up slowly, awestruck at the results of four dimes. Then the Magnificent Brain cleared and he remembered why they had dropped those dimes into the telephone. He looked up at the house. Not a light was shining.

Alvin Fernald walked out of the bushes, straight and proud, chest thrown out. A spotlight picked him up, then another. They were blinding, but Alvin walked steadily toward them.

From behind one of the lights he heard a voice say, "Why, it's that Fernald kid again. What's he up to now?"

Then his dad was standing in front of him, shielding him from the lights, and Shoie and the Pest were at his side.

"What's this all about, Alvin?" his dad said quietly, almost as though he were asking Alvin whether he'd mowed the lawn that afternoon. That was one of the many things Alvin liked about his father. He was always calm and collected, no matter what disaster threatened.

"There's a stranger in that house," said Alvin, pointing to the darkened windows. "It's the mysterious Mr. Smith. He's holding Mr. Link prisoner, and he has Mrs. Murphy locked in the basement. He's going to harm Mrs. Murphy unless Mr. Link solves the code and reads him the secret message."

"What secret message?" asked Sergeant Fernald patiently.

"The secret message about Miss Fenwick's buried treasure."

"All right, Alvin. I'm not sure what you're talking about, but you kids wait here while we find out what's going on." He looked around at all the men, vehicles, and equipment. By now, it seemed as though half the town was there, watching and listening. "When you holler for help, Alvin, you holler mighty loud."

Sergeant Fernald walked away and talked for a moment with Buford Jones, the other policeman, and the fire chief. Buford disappeared around to the back of the house. Then, at a signal from Sergeant Fernald, every spotlight swung around and lighted the front door. It was brighter than the dome of the state capitol.

There was a long wait. Nothing happened. Then the Sergeant started slowly up the front walk.

The Pest murmured, "What if that man has a gun?"

The thought made Alvin's pounding heart skip a beat.

Cautiously, Sergeant Fernald approached the house. Just as he put his foot on the bottom step, the front door opened slowly. An upraised hand emerged, then Mr. Smith's head, then the other hand. Clearly, in the crisp night air, the man called, "Don't shoot! I give up. I give up. Besides, you don't have anything on me."

The Sergeant leaped up the steps and slipped a handcuff over one upraised wrist. "We'll see about that as soon as we talk with Mr. Link," he said crisply.

Buford Jones came hurrying around the house, and Alvin's dad turned the prisoner over to him. A moment after he'd disappeared into the house, lights came on in the darkened rooms.

Alvin watched as Buford led Mr. Smith over to the squad car. Once, the man glanced up and saw the three kids standing there. A look of pure venom crossed his face, a look so terrifying that Alvin knew it would haunt his dreams.

Then Sergeant Fernald's head poked out the front door, and he was calling, "You kids come in here. There's someone who wants to talk to you."

They raced up the front walk and burst into the house. Dad motioned them into Mr. Link's room.

He was propped up as usual, gray mane flowing about his head, and Mrs. Murphy was adjusting the pillow behind his back just as though nothing had happened.

"Hi, kids," he said, waving at them, a big smile on his face. "It's a night to remember, isn't it?"

"Wow!" said Alvin. "We were afraid he was going to hurt you."

"Hurt you," echoed the Pest.

"At first, Alvin thought you were helping him," said Shoie.

Alvin wished Shoie hadn't said it. "Well, just for a minute I did," he said lamely.

"*He* thought I was going to help him, too. He appeared at the door, asking for me, and Mrs. Murphy showed him in here. He told me he was seeking help to break a coded message and had heard that I knew something about such things. Even though there was something about his manner I didn't like, I told him to sit down and we'd discuss it. When I asked him where he'd obtained the message, he became highly excited and said, in effect, it was none of my business. I told him that messages are put into code because they are secret, and that it is against my principles to try to solve a coded message without knowing where it came from. At that he became violent, seized Mrs. Murphy, locked her in the basement, and told me that unless I solved the code, he'd not only harm me but her, too. With her at his mercy, I couldn't take any chances, but I *could* stall for time, pretending to try to break the code. It was mighty lucky for me that you kids came along."

"Mighty lucky!" repeated the Pest.

"It was mighty smart of you to throw us a message out the window," said Alvin.

"I worried that you might have forgotten the code we set up for our private messages. I wrote in code in case our mysterious stranger saw what I was writing and knew I was trying to get help. At the moment I heaved it toward the window, I gave a long, silent prayer that my pitching arm was still good."

Sergeant Fernald broke in. "What's all this about a secret message and Miss Fenwick's buried treasure?"

Alvin jumped as though he'd been stabbed with a pin. In the excitement, he'd forgotten all about solving the code and reading the treasure message.

"I solved it!" he shouted. "I broke the code! I know right where the treasure is hidden, out in Treasure Bluffs!"

"Let's go," said Shoie, starting for the door. "Let's go trind that feasure."

"Whoa," said Sergeant Fernald. "Wait a minute. We've had enough excitement for one night. Even if you *have* learned where the treasure is buried, we can't go stumbling around out there in the darkness. We'll go in the morning."

A groan went up from all three kids.

"Plllleeeeease, Daddy," coaxed the Pest.

"No, not tonight. You belong in bed right now."

Just then Mrs. Murphy came walking through the doorway, a tray in her hands. "Perhaps the children belong in bed, Sergeant Fernald. But I'll bet they have just time enough for some cookies and milk."

She winked at the Sergeant and offered him the cookies first.

CHAPTER 12

The Secret of the Buried Treasure

ALVIN came awake in an instant.

When he had crawled into bed the night before, thoughts of Mr. Smith, secret codes, and buried treasure were churning through his head in such a jumble that the Magnificent Brain flashed all kinds of short circuits. He hadn't believed he'd be able to sleep a wink. But he had fallen asleep the moment his head touched the pillow.

Now, sunbeams were dancing in the bright light streaming through the window, and he had no idea what time it was. He glanced up at the old cuckoo clock on the wall, mentally subtracted an hour and ten minutes, and discovered it was 9:15. He'd found the old clock in Mrs. Otto's trash can, had taken it home, and found that it gained exactly thirty-five minutes a day. He'd proudly hung it on the wall. Every three days, first thing in the morning, he'd reset the hands. After that, the first morning he'd subtract thirty-five minutes, the second morning seventy minutes, and the third morning one hundred five minutes. He'd done it for so long now that he could tell at a glance almost exactly what time it was when he woke up each morning.

9:15! Leaping out of bed, he raced for the bathroom. He ran some water into the wash basin, dipped his fingertips into it, touched them to his cheeks, then rubbed the towel across his face. Quickly, he brushed his teeth. Back in his room, he pulled on a T-shirt and a pair of jeans.

His mother and father and the Pest had already finished breakfast and were sitting at the table talking.

"Darn it!" said Alvin. "Why didn't you wake me up? Let's go find the treasure!"

"Slow down, son. Slow down." His father motioned toward Alvin's chair. "Sit down and have some breakfast. You can't go treasure hunting on an empty stomach. You were pretty tired last night, after all that excitement, so we decided to let you sleep."

"Let you sleep," repeated the Pest. "I was up at six o'clock."

"But somebody might beat us to the treasure," groaned Alvin, as his mother put a plate of bacon and eggs on the table.

"Nobody knows anything about where to find that treasure but you, Alvin," said his dad. "Matter of fact, I only have your word that *you* know where to find it. However, I did have a long talk down at the jail with Mr. Smith last night, after you'd gone to bed."

"What did he say?" asked Alvin, his voice muffled in a bite of toast.

"Oh, he talked. Plenty. The fact that he's behind bars completely loosened his tongue. He seemed glad enough to spill the whole story. And, apparently, there *is* a treasure—or at least was one—because his story jibes with what Miss Fenwick told us. It seems that Blacky Blackwell, the bushwhacker and former spy, was Mr. Smith's great-great uncle, or some such relative. Incidentally, his name isn't really Smith, but Hitchcock.

"Anyway, Hitchcock grew up in a very old house that had been in the family for several generations. Apparently it was the same house where Blacky was found by the Army patrol. Maybe you remember that Blacky was killed in the home of a relative, after he'd murdered Mr. Moses."

"How did Hitchcock find out about the treasure?" asked Alvin.

"About a year ago he was poking around up in the attic and saw the corner of a yellowed scrap of paper sticking out between two boards. When he unfolded it, he found the coded message. Curious, he went back through the family records and uncovered the story of Blacky. He guessed—apparently correctly—that the message told where to find the treasure from the

Fenwick plantation. He had no luck solving the code, and over a period of months it became an obsession with him. Finally, because he knew Blacky had passed through Riverton just before he got rid of the treasure, he came here. And it was from here, in desperation, that he finally wrote Miss Fenwick."

"He's a mighty spooky man," said the Pest.

"He's a man to be pitied," corrected her father. "Of course, he'll stand trial for holding Mr. Link and Mrs. Murphy prisoner. But he's thought so much about that treasure that he has become unbalanced, in my opinion."

"He's daffy," said the Pest.

"That's one way to describe it. You know, he *still* thinks that treasure is rightfully his, simply because one of his ancestors stole it."

Alvin put the last forkful of eggs in his mouth. "Let's go," he said, standing up.

"Don't be surprised at what you see outside," said his mom. "By now, the whole town has heard about the treasure."

Alvin grabbed his jacket and opened the front door. He stopped dead in his tracks. Cars were parked in both directions as far as he could see. On the front lawn, people were gathered in little knots, talking. Fire Chief McReynolds was there with a shovel in his hands, chatting with Shoie and Miss Fenwick. On the front walk stood Mr. Bronski, the reporter from the *Riverton News*, beside a photographer, who had heard the front door open and now was peering through his camera at Alvin. Mrs. Petrus was there, leaning on her crutches—she hadn't been out of the house in months —and down on the next corner was Mrs. Dinwiddie, holding her brand new baby. Mr. Pinkney was standing beside the curb, wearing hiking boots. Milling about on the lawn next door was an entire pack of uniformed Cub Scouts. And across the street stood Mr. Ogilvie, proudly talking to a group of excited neighbors.

When Alvin saw Mr. Ogilvie, he slammed the door shut and ran back upstairs, ignoring his father's puzzled glance. In his room, he quickly squirmed under the bed, his back to the floor, and slid out the matchbox he had nailed to the underside of one of the slats. He took four dimes from the coins inside the box, dashed back downstairs, and opened the door. A flashbulb popped. The Cub Scouts started shouting, and people began climbing into their cars. Alvin ran across to Mr. Ogilvie.

"Here's the forty cents I owe you," he said. "Thanks, Mr. Ogilvie." He turned and ran back across the street.

The family crowded into the police car, along with Shoie and Miss Fenwick. Sergeant Fernald turned on the siren as soon as he pulled away from the curb. Alvin tried to be nonchalant about the siren, but it was a big thrill riding in the patrol car, especially with the siren growling. His dad normally didn't let him ride in the patrol car because it was for "official business only," but apparently finding buried treasure was official business.

As they passed through the business district, Alvin looked through the back window. Forty or fifty cars paraded behind them, and as he watched, a big trailer truck that had been delivering furniture to Billings' Department Store pulled right into the middle of the procession, horn blaring, with Mr. Billings running alongside and finally leaping into the cab.

On the corner of Maple Street another siren answered the one on the patrol car, and Alvin saw an ambulance pull into the procession just behind them. He was startled. "What's the ambulance for?"

"Mr. Link and Mrs. Murphy are inside," replied his dad. "We made arrangements for the ambulance to pick them up. I figured they might like to see the end of the story."

At the city limits they headed down the county road that ran along the river. Ahead, across the farm fields, Alvin could see the land rise toward the bluffs. His heart began to beat a little faster. What if this whole thing were a flop? What if there *weren't* any treasure? Or what if someone, years ago, had found it?

At the top of the bluffs, Sergeant Fernald pulled into the parking space beside the old picnic tables. Behind them, cars stretched for a half-mile down the road. There was a clatter of doors slamming, and excited shouts. When Alvin climbed out, the people began gathering around.

"All right, Alvin," said his dad quietly. "Lead the way. Where's the treasure?"

Alvin tried to swallow, but his throat wouldn't seem to work properly. "We'll head down by the river," he said, his voice so tight it was screechy. He led the way down the wooded trail.

At the bottom of the slope he headed upriver until he came to a pool of still water, fed by hillside springs, that flowed gently into the river. Here, he stopped and drew the coded message from his pocket.

"This is the start of the treasure trail," he announced.

"How do you know?" asked Mr. Bronski, taking notes for his story in the *Riverton News*.

"It says so in this message," said Alvin, staring at the paper in his hand.

Mr. Bronski took a look at the paper. "Looks like a mishmash of letters to me."

A flashbulb popped.

"It's a very simple code," said Alvin. "All you need is the key."

"How did you find the key?" Mr. Bronski had raised his voice so all the other folks could hear.

"I did just what Mr. Link told me to. I kept thinking about Blacky and what he was doing when he put this message into code. He was in a hurry because he had to catch Mr. Moses, who was the only other person who knew where the treasure was buried. He didn't have *time* to work out a complicated code. Even a simple substitution code would have taken too long. Besides, I ran a letter-frequency count, and it appeared that no substitution was involved. Therefore, I assumed that the original letters in the code stood for themselves."

Alvin looked up. There was a look not only of puzzlement but of awe on the faces of everyone around him, all except his father, who had a proud smile on his face.

"I tried to put myself in Blacky's place, to figure out what I would do if I were faced with this problem. I'd need a very simple code that I could write out quickly. Finally, I decided what I'd do and I tried it. It worked."

At that moment a thought raced through his mind. The thought seemed to travel back through time for more than a century, and intersected the thoughts of a savage bushwhacker. How exciting, he mused, to touch the mind of someone else, far removed in time and space, by means of reading his code.

Alvin said aloud, "I can read the instructions on finding the treasure right off this piece of paper, without even rewriting it."

Mr. Bronski took the paper carefully from his hand. The letters were smudged, but could still be read clearly:

SREWO TETIN ARGNE EWTEB GIDDN ASECA
PELVE WTTHG IRNRU TKCOR DAEHE LTRUT
OTHTR ONOGT SEWHT RONTS EWSEC APNEE

TFIFO   GREDL   UOBEG   RALMO   RFFFU   LBTSE
PEETS   FOESA   BTALO   OPRET   AWRAE   LCDNI
FSFFU   LBREV   IROTS   ELIME   ERHTT   SEWHT
UOSEK   IRTSA   NAIDN   INOTR   EVIRD   ELLAC
EGALL   IVOTO   GXXXX

"I can't read it at all," said Mr. Bronski in a baffled voice.

"Try reading it *backward*, starting with the last letter," said Alvin triumphantly. He took the paper from Mr. Bronski and began to read. "Go to village called Riverton, Indiana. Strike southwest three miles to river bluffs. Find clear-water pool at base of steepest bluff." He paused, his voice shaking a little. "That's where we are now, at the clear-water pool."

"At the clear-water pool," repeated the Pest eagerly, as though she had read the message many times.

"Go on," said Sergeant Fernald.

Alvin started reading again. "From large boulder"— he pointed toward a huge rock that lay half-buried beside the pool. "That's the biggest boulder around here, so I guess we start there."

He scrambled up to the top of the boulder, and continued reading. "From large boulder, go fifteen paces west northwest." A look of dismay crossed his face. "I forgot to bring a compass."

"Here's one!" piped up a shrill voice from the crowd. It was one of the Cub Scouts, and the crowd, lifting him high above their heads, passed him up beside

Alvin. The boy held his compass as seriously as if the fate of the world were in his hands, until the needle stopped wiggling. Carefully, he turned the compass until the directions were right, then dramatically pointed. "That's west northwest!" he shouted.

Alvin climbed down from the boulder and took fifteen steps in the direction the boy had pointed. He deliberately made his steps big, trying to imitate the strides of a grown man. Then, he stopped and began reading again.

"Go north to turtle-head rock." He looked north. Sure enough, there was a boulder, a little way up the slope of the bluff, that looked like a turtle with its head upraised. From any other direction it would look like just another rock. Alvin scrambled over to it, the crowd streaming along behind.

He read the final sentence of the coded message. "Turn right twelve paces and dig between granite towers."

Turning himself a quarter-turn to his right, he started counting off the steps. Before he was halfway through the count, he saw the granite towers, two large spires of rock, similar in shape and almost the same height, dead ahead. He didn't even bother to count the last steps. Standing smack between the towering rocks, he announced, "We dig here."

Chief McReynolds came hurrying up, the shovel still in his hands. He put the blade of the shovel into the rocky soil and started digging.

It was hard going. The shovel kept biting into small rocks that had to be pried out, one at a time. After five minutes the Chief stood up, the perspiration running down his forehead and into his eyes. Sergeant Fernald took over the shovel.

The crowd had grown quiet now. Every eye was on the hole as it grew larger and deeper. Finally, the Sergeant, too, stopped to rest. By now, the hole was three feet deep, and there was no sign of any treasure. While Sergeant Fernald was resting, Shoie grabbed the shovel and began scrabbling awkwardly through the dirt. Now and then a shovelful of gravel flew out of the hole.

Alvin's stomach began to do flip-flops when it appeared that no treasure was to be found. He re-read the coded message. He was *sure* that he'd followed the instructions exactly.

Now the crowd was growing restless. Alvin heard someone mutter something about "that kid leading us on a wild goose chase." A look of extreme disappointment had crept into Miss Fenwick's normally smiling eyes.

Alvin quietly folded the message and put it in his pocket. At that moment Shoie whispered, in a voice too low for the others to hear, "Quick, K-21 1/2. I hit something with the shovel!"

Alvin leaped into the hole beside him. There, just beside the tip of the shovel, was a half-covered and rotten board. The shovel moved once and exposed a rusty hinge.

The boys leaned over so quickly that they bumped heads. It was a jarring bump that hurt like sixty, but neither of them could be bothered just now. Down on their hands and knees they went, scooping out the dirt and small stones with their fingers. A handful of dirt sailed over Alvin's shoulder and he heard an "Ugh!" from above. Glancing up, he saw Chief McReynolds rubbing gravel out of his eyes. Alvin didn't even pause in his digging.

Two minutes later the boys had half-uncovered the old chest. In places the wood was so rotten it crumbled beneath their fingers. Alvin leaned over and pushed down on the top board. Suddenly, it gave way and, losing his balance, he tumbled forward head first to find himself with his head caught *inside* the treasure chest. Shoie pulled him back to his feet.

Alvin's fall had caved in the last of the rotting wood. His eyes almost popped out of his head at the sight at his feet.

The treasure!

Inside the chest was old silver, long tarnished but still gleaming faintly: knives, forks, and spoons intricately fashioned in a beautiful old design; pitchers, cups, and platters of solid silver; silver napkin rings by the dozens, and gold-inlaid inkwells and letter openers.

In one corner of the chest was the remains of an old leather bag, its contents now spilled out and mixed with the silver: brooches and rings, necklaces and lockets, bracelets and pins. Jewels gleamed in the gold, gleamed so brightly that they seemed to have stored, for more than a century, their beauty for this moment.

In another corner of the chest, Alvin saw strange coins by the dozens, jumbled into a great hodgepodge of treasure.

Shoie was the first to speak. "Wow!" was all he could say, in a whisper.

"Wow!" repeated the Pest.

Alvin looked up at the ring of faces. His father's face looked proudly down, not at the treasure, but at him. Next to him was Miss Fenwick's face, tears forming in her eyes.

Alvin finally found his voice. "Well, that's that," he said briskly. "There's your treasure." He climbed out of the hole.

The people were jammed so close around that he could hardly get his breath. They crowded in, shouting and waving their arms, until no one could move. Miss Fenwick almost fainted, either from the sight of her family's ancient treasure or from the press of the crowd. Finally, Sergeant Fernald made everyone line up and file past the hole. Each took a long startled look inside, then stared admiringly at Alvin.

Now that he had found his voice, Alvin pretended to be all business. "Well, we'd better take care of this old treasure. What do you think we should do with it, Dad?"

After a moment's thought, his dad said, "I'll ask

Chief McReynolds to guard it while we go up and get the emergency blankets out of the squad car. We'll put all the treasure in the blankets, take it back to the squad car, and drive it to the bank. It'll be safe there."

By the time they reached the top of the hill, Alvin was out of breath, either from exertion or excitement. Waiting in a parking space by the top of the trail was the ambulance. Inside, Mr. Link and Mrs. Murphy were talking to the newspaper reporter, who had climbed in beside the driver.

Alvin, Shoie, and the Pest walked over to the ambulance.

"Hi, Mr. Link!" said Alvin.

"Hello, Agent K-21 1/2," said Mr. Link. "I haven't seen so much excitement in years. You certainly did a fine job of breaking that code."

Alvin didn't reply. He just looked at the ground, trying to be modest.

The Fernalds, and Miss Fenwick walked up. Many others, too, had come up the trail, and clustered around the ambulance.

Mr. Bronski cleared his throat and said loudly, "Well, Alvin, how about an interview for the *Riverton News*? You found that treasure, so I suppose it's yours. What are you going to do with it?"

"Whoa," said Sergeant Fernald quickly. "Not so fast. I know enough about the law to know that the courts will have to decide who owns that treasure. Until then, nobody knows."

"Right," said Mr. Bronski. "But I remember a couple of cases where money was found buried in the ground. In those cases it was awarded to the finder." He smiled happily at Alvin.

When Alvin cleared his throat everybody stopped talking. There was a long moment of silence. A flashbulb popped.

"I don't know who owns this treasure," said Alvin. "But if it's mine, because I found it, I know what I'll do with it."

"What?" asked Mr. Bronski, his pencil poised.

Alvin Fernald, Secret Agent and Cryptographer, took a deep breath, then said in a ringing voice, "I'll return it where it belongs, to the place it came from. I'll give it to Miss Fenwick to take back to the orphanage with her. She can sell it, if she wants, and use the money to take care of all the kids down there. I think the money would do more good there than anywhere else." He looked at the tips of his dusty shoes.

There was such a long silence that Alvin finally looked up to see what was the matter. The first face he noted was Miss Fenwick's, and this time the tears were streaming down her face, making long shiny lines on her cheeks.

Then someone back in the crowd started to clap, and soon the bluffs across the river were echoing back the cheers.

Alvin looked over at Shoie. "Q-3, I hope you agree

with what I said about the treasure."

"Right, old bean. You vet my gote. I mean you get my vote."

Alvin turned to the Pest. "How about you?"

"Right, old bean," she echoed.

"I thought you'd feel that way," said Alvin Fernald softly. "You're a couple of top agents, Q-3 and—uh—uh— Secret Agent Z-13 1/4."

"Oh, Alvin!" said the Pest.

He knew he had given her the finest of medals.

Appendix

Secrets from Alvin's Master Code Room

If you walked into Alvin's code room (which, of course, is impossible because of his burglar alarm to keep out the Pest), you'd see a strange sight. It looks as though the walls have measles. Each "meez" (which is what the Pest calls a measle spot) is a scrap of paper thumbtacked to the wall. On some scraps are notes about codes and ciphers; on others are practice messages to cipher and decipher. These scraps represent much of what Alvin has learned in his study of codes. If you study his notes, and practice encoding and decoding messages, you'll soon find that you, too, can be a "Secret Agent and Master Criptogruffer."

Codes

In a CODE, a word or a symbol stands for a complete thought. Example: GLIMP or 🐟 can mean, "I will meet you in the clubhouse." ZOUND or 🐟 can mean "two p.m." Then GLIMP ZOUND, or 🐟 🐟 means, "I will meet you in the clubhouse at two p.m." Codes require at least two code books, one for the sender and one for the receiver. *Warning: Enemy agents may try to obtain these code books!*

Ciphers

In a CIPHER, each letter, number, or symbol stands for *one letter of the alphabet.* Examples: 1 stands for A, 2 stands for B, etc.; C stands for A, D stands for B, etc.; 丌 stands for A, Δ stands for B, etc. Thus, codes can only be used to send thoughts that are already in the code book, but ciphers can be used to send any message, because a cipher consists of a complete alphabet.

Definitions

ENCODE means to put a message into code.

ENCIPHER means to put a message into cipher.

DECODE means to translate a message from code to English.

DECIPHER means to translate a message from cipher to English.

A CRYPTOGRAPHER is a man who works with codes or ciphers.

CRYPTANALYSIS is the process of breaking a secret code.

A NULL is a meaningless letter in a ciphered message, placed there either to fill out the number of units in the message or to confuse the enemy if he tries to decipher the message.

Alvin Fernald's Symbol Cipher

This is the cipher which I invented and which Mr. Link broke. Its weakness is that it is difficult to memorize and fairly easy to break.

A	⅃	J	(	S	○
B	[	K	‿	T	φ
C	⌐	L	⌒	U	⊖
D	⌐·	M	▭	V	⚲
E	✕	N	⊟·	W	⊶
F	✕·	O	▯	X	⚲
G	✕.	P	⊞	Y	⊷
H	✕	Q	▷	Z	⊗
I	⊃	R	◺		

Practice message to encipher in Alvin Fernald's Symbol Cipher:

BEWARE OF GOOEY LARSON. HE HAS SPITBALLS.

Practice message to decipher in Alvin Fernald's Symbol Cipher:

Shoie's Special Cipher for Secretaries

Shoie developed this one, using only the keys on the typewriter.

A	"	J	*	S	,
B	#	K	-	T	=
C	$	L	:	U	+
D	%	M	;	V	/-
E	_	N	@	W	-?
F	&	O	¢	X	/-/
G	'	P	?	Y	/+
H	(	Q	/	Z	($
I	)	R	.		

146

Shoie invented a pretty good cipher here, but it's difficult to memorize.

Practice message to encipher in Shoie's cipher:

PUT ON YOUR BEARD. WE'VE BEEN RECOGNIZED.

Practice message to decipher in Shoie's cipher:

) :) - _ . " , ? # _ . . /+

" @ " @ " ;) : - , (" - _ ,

Secret Agent Z-13 1/4's Alphabet Box

This is the Pest's favorite.

	1	2	3	4	5
1	A	B	C	D	E
2	F	G	H	I	J
3	K	L	M	N	O
4	P	Q	R	S	T
5	U	V	W or X	Y	Z

To use this cipher, first find the letter you want, then write down the number to the left and the number above. A, for example, is 11; B is 12; R is 43. Use a hyphen between numbers and a space between words.

This cipher is easy to redraw from memory. Even Gooey Larson could remember it.

Practice message to encipher with the Alphabet Box:

PLEASE MOVE. YOU ARE STANDING ON MY TOE.

Practice message to decipher with the Alphabet Box:

24 41-51-45   24-45-13-23-24-34-22
41-35-53-14-15-43   35-34   44-11-32-32-54-44
25-11-13-31-15-45

Civil War Cipher

Miss Fenwick says that this cipher was used by Northern prisoners of war, held in Southern prisons, to smuggle messages to friends on the outside.

First, memorize the diagrams above. Then, use only the lines of the diagram to represent the letters:

A ⌐	F ⊏	K ⟩	P ⊡	U ⋔	X ⟩
B ⊔	G ⊓	L ⟨	Q ⊒	V ⌐	Y ⟨
C ⌐	H ⋒	M ∧	R ⊡	W ∨	Z ∧
D ⊐	I ⌐	N ⊔	S ⊑		
E ◻	J ∨	O ⊔	T ⊓		

The four tic-tac-toe diagrams are easy to remember, so this code can be redrawn at any time.

Practice message to encipher in the Civil War Cipher:

> STAY IN YOUR SEAT. YOUR PANTS ARE
> TORN.

Practice message to decipher in the Civil War Cipher:

⟨⊡⊓⊑ ∧⌐⟩⊐ ⌐ ⊑⊔⊔∨

⊏⊔⊔⊓ ⌐⊏⊓⊐◻ ⊑⌐⋒⊔⊔⟨

Alvin Fernald's Cipher Sticks

Use two pieces of cardboard (or strips of light wood), one twice as long as the other. Divide the shorter one into twenty-six equal spaces, the longer one into fifty-two spaces the same size as those on the shorter stick. Then, print the alphabet on both sticks like this:

```
┌─────────────────────────────────────────┐
│ABCDEFGHIJKLMNOPQRSTUVWXYZ│
└─────────────────────────────────────────┘
```
```
┌──────────────────────────────────────────────────────┐
│ABCDEFGHIJKLMNOPQRSTUVWXYZABCDEFGHIJ etc.│
└──────────────────────────────────────────────────────┘
```

The cipher sticks permit you to change your cipher each day. For example, Shoie and I may agree that tomorrow we'll use the "M" cipher. Tomorrow, when I want to send a message, I'll place the A on the shorter stick above the M on the longer stick. Then A=M, B=N, C=O, etc.

When Shoie receives the message, he places the A on his shorter stick over M just as I did. Then, if the letter M appears in my message, he finds M on his longer stick, looks directly above, and knows that it really is an A.

The day after tomorrow we may agree to use the "P" cipher. Then, we'll place the A on the shorter stick directly above the P on the longer stick, and we're ready to encipher or decipher messages in the "P" cipher.

The two sticks give us twenty-six different ciphers, a different cipher for almost every day of the month!

Practice message to encipher in the "K" cipher:

LOOK OUT. MISS PEPPERSMITH IS SUSPI-CIOUS.

Practice message to decipher in the "X" cipher:

JBBQ JB YV QEB DLIACFPE FK QEB AFJB PQLOB

Alvin Fernald's Master Code Wheel

Use a sheet of thin paper to trace off the two circles shown below:

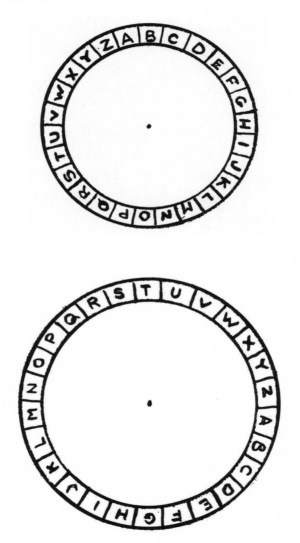

Now, use a piece of carbon paper to transfer the circles to stiff paper or cardboard, and cut them out. Thumbtack both circles to a small board, and turn them until they spin freely.

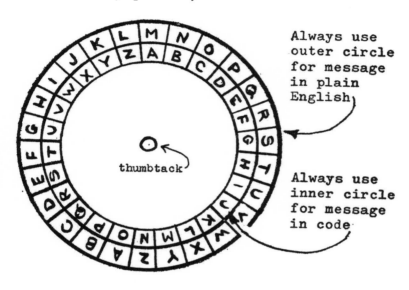

Always use outer circle for message in plain English

Always use inner circle for message in code

If Shoie and I have agreed, beforehand, to use the "G" cipher today, I turn the *inner* circle until the G lines up with A in the *outer* circle. Then, I encipher the message, finding the original letters on the outer circle and writing down the corresponding code letters from the inner circle. When Shoie receives the message, he sets his master cipher wheel for the "G" cipher, just as I did. Then, he looks up the ciphered letters from the message on the inner circle, and writes down the letters on the outer circle, to put the message back into plain English.

In effect, this Master Code Wheel bends my Cipher Sticks around in a circle.

Practice message to encipher in "G" cipher:

ALL THE PEEVEY KIDS HAVE
CONNECTED TOES.

Practice message to decipher in "Q" cipher:

CO REECUHQDW IQYBUT JXHEKWX CHI
ZEXDIEDI MYDTEM.

Using a Key Word with a Cipher Wheel

Wow! This is a good one. I'll bet nobody but Mr. Link could decipher this one.

To use this system, Shoie and I first agree on a secret word, what we call a key word. We use any word, as long as it doesn't have the same letter twice. *Thumb* and *nose* are good key words, but not *knee* or *throat*.

Suppose I want to send Shoie the following message:

GIVE ME A LEMON DROP.

I simply copy off the key word beneath the message, repeating it over and over again. It doesn't make any difference whether the key word is complete at the end of the message. In this case our key word is *nose*.

GIVE ME A LEMON DROP
NOSE NO S ENOSE NOSE.

Now, I use my cipher wheel. First, I set it to the "N" code, because that is the first letter of the key word. (To do this, remember, I put the N on the inner circle opposite the A on the outer circle.) With the cipher wheel set for the "N" code, I encipher all the letters that appear just above the N's:

```
GIVE   ME  A  LEMON  DROP.
NOSE   NO  S  ENOSE  NOSE
T      Z      R      Q     .
```

Then, I change the cipher wheel to the "O" cipher, and encipher all the letters that appear above the O's:

```
GIVE   ME  A  LEMON  DROP.
NOSE   NO  S  ENOSE  NOSE
TW     ZS     RA     QF    .
```

I do the same with the "S" and the "E" ciphers. My sheet of paper finally looks like this:

```
G I VE   ME   A  LEMON  DROP
NO SE    NO   S  ENOSE  NOSE
TWNI     ZS   S  PRAGR  QFGT
```

The last line, of course, is the enciphered message that I send to Shoie.

The combination of the key word and the cipher wheel is wonderful. In my original message, GIVE ME A LEMON DROP, there are three E's. In the enciphered message, the three E's have become an I, an S, and an R. That kind of a mess would be hard for even Mr. Link to solve!

When Shoie gets the message, he repeats the key word beneath it:

```
TWNI  ZS  S  PRAGR  QFGT
NOSE  NO  S  ENOS E  NOSE
```

Then, he sets his cipher wheel for the "N" cipher, and deciphers all the letters that appear above the N's:

```
TWNI  ZS  K  PRAGR  QFGT
NOSE  NO  S  ENOS E  NOSE
G         M  E         D
```

He does the same thing with the "O," "S," and "E" ciphers.

By now I'm so hungry that I've gone to get my own lemon drop.

I can hardly wait to try *this* one on Gooey Larson!

Breaking Enemy Ciphers

Here's some stuff that helps to break enemy ciphers.

E is more frequently used than any other letter. Then come T, A, O, and N. The complete letter Frequency Table is:

ETAONRISHDLFCMUGYPWBVKXJQZ.

The first five letters of the Frequency Table make up forty-five percent of the letters used in the English language. The first nine letters of the Frequency Table make up seventy percent of all the letters used in the English language.

Several combinations of letters appear frequently in words. The most common combinations, reading down the columns, are:

TH	EN
HE	OF
AN	TE
RE	ED
ER	OR
IN	TI
ON	HI
AT	AS
ND	TO
ST	WH
ES	

Many letters are frequently doubled. The most common are:

LL	FF
EE	RR
SS	NN
OO	PP
TT	CC

There are two one-letter words: A and I.
The most common two letter words are:

OF	HE
TO	BY
IN	OR
IT	ON
IS	DO
BE	IF
AS	ME
AT	MY
SO	UP
WE	AN

Be a criptogruffer! Here is a practice message to analyze and decipher:

L NQRZ ZKHUH WKHUH LV D ZKROH
EDWFK RI URWWHQ WRPDWRHV. LI DQ
HQHPB DJHQW ILQGV WKH FOXEKRXVH
ZH ZLOO DWWDFN ZLWK WKHP.

DOYLQ

Hints:
This is a letter-substitution cipher.
Use the Frequency Table.
Note the one-letter words.
Note the apparent signature.
Note letter combinations ZK and WK

Copy the message in large print on a separate sheet of paper. At the bottom of the sheet, write the alphabet. As soon as you *think* you know what a letter is, but aren't sure, put it *beneath* the corresponding letter of the alphabet. When you are *sure* you know what a letter is, put it *above* the corresponding letter of the alphabet and fill it in wherever it occurs in the message.

Scytales

Make scytales from dowels, old mop handles, or anything else that you can find around the house. WARNING! *Don't ever use Mom's mop handle without getting her okay first!* The time I made scytales from her mop handle, which I took without permission, I had to spend three weeks' allowance on a new mop.

DON'T YOU EVER DO THIS!

Cut two wooden rods to approximately the same length, one for you and one for a friend or whoever is going to be receiving messages. Use a long ribbon of paper about half an inch wide. (Cut a sheet of paper into long narrow strips and tape them together.) Wind the ribbon spirally on the scytale, so that each turn of the paper comes just to the edge of the previous turn. Tape will help hold the ends in place. Then write the message down the length of the scytale, turning the stick a little for each new line. When you're through, take the paper ribbon off the scytale.

The writing won't make any sense to an enemy agent, even if the ribbon falls into his hands. When your friend gets the message, he wraps it spirally around his scytale and he can read the message clearly.

My most important message to Shoie on a scytale was:

AGENT Q-3: BEWARE OF MOP HANDLES UNTIL YOU DISCUSS THEIR USE WITH PROPER AUTHORITIES. AGENT K-21 1/2

Good Book!

Best book on codes that I, Secret Agent K-21 1/2, have found is a neat book titled *Codes and Secret Writing*. It was written by Herbert S. Zim and published by William Morrow & Company, Inc. Miss Jackson showed it to me at the library, and I liked it so well I ordered a copy at the bookstore. It's full of zillions of good codes and ciphers, and it's written for kids about my age. There are several mysterious messages it's fun to decipher. There's even a special section on secret inks that you can make out of stuff around the house or that you can get at the drug store!

About the Author

CLIFFORD B. HICKS was born and raised in a town in Iowa much like Riverton, the scene of *Alvin's Secret Code* and *The Marvelous Inventions of Alvin Fernald*. He began writing professionally during his high-school years, when he was a correspondent for the Des Moines *Register and Tribune*. During World War II, Mr. Hicks served as a Major in the Marine Corps on Guam and Bougainville. In the service he learned something about codes and ciphers, a subject he had studied briefly in college. After the war Mr. Hicks joined the staff of *Popular Mechanics* magazine, eventually becoming Editor-in-Chief of the magazine and its seven foreign editions. He graduated *cum laude* from Northwestern University. Two of his juvenile books have been made into Disney movies.

Mr. Hicks now lives in the mountains of western North Carolina. He spends his leisure time hiking, reading, woodworking; and, yes, a bit of writing.